identity

Books by Milan Kundera

The Joke

Laughable Loves

Life Is Elsewhere

Farewell Waltz
(EARLIER TRANSLATION: *The Farewell Party*)

The Book of Laughter and Forgetting

The Unbearable Lightness of Being

Immortality

Slowness

Identity

Jacques and His Master (PLAY)

The Art of the Novel (ESSAY)

Testaments Betrayed (ESSAY)

MILAN KUNDERA

identity

Translated from the French by Linda Asher

HarperFlamingo

An Imprint of HarperCollins*Publishers*

FIRST EDITION

Designed by Elina D. Nudelman

Library of Congress Cataloging-in-Publication Data

Kundera, Milan.
[Identité. English]
Identity : a novel / Milan Kundera ; translated from the French by Linda Asher.
p.   cm.
ISBN 0-06-017564-8
I. Asher, Linda.   II. Title.
PQ2671.U47I3413   1998
891.8'68354—dc21   97-31907

98 99 00 01 02 ❖/RRD 10 9 8 7 6 5 4 3 2

1

A hotel in a small town on the Normandy coast, which they found in a guidebook. Chantal got there Friday night and would spend a night alone, without Jean-Marc, who was to join her on Saturday around noon. She left a small valise in the room, went outside, and, after a short stroll through unfamiliar streets, returned to the hotel's own dining room. At seven-thirty, the restaurant was still empty. She sat down at a table and waited for someone to notice her. At the far side of the room, near the door to the kitchen, two waitresses were deep in discussion. Since she hated to raise her voice, Chantal got up, crossed the room, and stopped beside them; but they were too absorbed by their topic: "I'm telling you, it's ten years already. I know them. It's terrible. And there's not a trace. None. It was on TV." The other one: "What could have happened to him?" "Nobody can even imagine. And that's what's horrible." "A murder?" "They looked everywhere." "A kidnapping?" "But who would do that? And why? He wasn't a rich guy, or important. They

1

showed them all on TV. His children, his wife. It's heartbreaking. Do you realize?"

Then she noticed Chantal: "You know that program on TV about people who've disappeared? *Lost to Sight*, it's called."

"Yes," said Chantal.

"Maybe you saw what happened to the Bourdieu family. They're from here."

"Yes, it's awful," said Chantal, unsure how to turn talk of a tragedy to the mundane issue of food.

"You want dinner," said the other waitress finally.

"Yes."

"I'll get the headwaiter. Go have a seat."

Her colleague went on: "Can you imagine, someone you love disappears and you never find out what happened to him! It could drive you insane!"

Chantal returned to her table; it took five minutes for the headwaiter to come over; she ordered a cold meal, very simple; she didn't like to eat alone; ah, how she hated that, eating alone!

She sliced the ham on her plate and could not still the thoughts the waitresses had stirred up in her: in a world where our every move is monitored and recorded, where in department stores cameras watch you, where people constantly jostle you, where a person cannot even make love without being quizzed the next day by researchers and poll-takers ("Where do you make love?" "How many times a week?" "With or without a condom?"), how is it possible that someone could slip out of surveillance and disappear without a trace? Yes, she certainly does know that program with its terrifying title, *Lost to Sight*, the only program that undoes her with its genuineness, its sadness, as if an intervention from some other realm has forced television to give up all its frivolity; in grave tones, the host appeals to the audience to come forward with any evidence that could help find the missing person. At the end of the program they show pictures, one after the other, of all the *Lost to Sight* people discussed in previous programs; some have been unfindable for as long as eleven years.

She imagines losing Jean-Marc that way someday. Never knowing, reduced to imagining anything and everything. She could not even kill herself, because suicide would be a betrayal, a refusal to wait, a loss of patience. She would be

condemned to live until the end of her days in
unrelenting horror.

2

She went up to her room, fell asleep with diffi-
culty, and woke in the middle of the night after a
long dream. It was populated exclusively by fig-
ures from her past: her mother (long dead) and,
mainly, her former husband (she had not seen
him for years, and he looked different, as if the
director of the dream had made a bad casting
choice); he was there with his overbearing, ener-
getic sister and with his new wife (Chantal had
never seen her; nonetheless, in the dream, she had
no doubt about her identity); at the end, he made
Chantal some vague erotic propositions, and his
new wife kissed her hard on the mouth and tried
to slip her tongue between Chantal's lips. Tongues
licking each other had always disgusted her. In
fact, that kiss was what woke her up.

Her discomfort from the dream was so extreme
that she went to some effort to figure out the reason for it. What troubled her so, she thinks, is the

dream's effect of nullifying the present. For she is passionately attached to her present; nothing in the world would induce her to trade it for the past or the future. That is why she dislikes dreams: they impose an unacceptable equivalence among the various periods of the same life, a leveling contemporaneity of everything a person has ever experienced; they discredit the present by denying it its privileged status. As in that night's dream: it obliterated a whole chunk of her life: Jean-Marc, their shared apartment, all the years they've spent together; in its place the past came lumbering in, people she broke off with long ago and who tried to capture her in the net of a banal sexual seduction. She felt on her mouth the wet lips of a woman (not an ugly woman—the dream's director had been fairly demanding in his choice of actress), and the sensation was so disagreeable that in the middle of the night she went to the bathroom to gargle and wash out her mouth for a long time.

3

F. was a very old friend of Jean-Marc's, they had known each other since high school; they had the same opinions, they got along well, and they stayed in touch until the day, several years back, when Jean-Marc suddenly and definitively turned against him and stopped seeing him. When he learned that F. was very ill in a hospital in Brussels, he had no wish to visit him, but Chantal insisted he go.

The sight of the old friend was shattering: he still remembered him as he had been in high school, a delicate boy, always perfectly turned out, endowed with a natural refinement beside which Jean-Marc felt like a rhinoceros. The subtle, effeminate features that used to make F. look younger than his age now made him look older: his face seemed grotesquely small, shriveled, wrinkled, like the mummified head of an Egyptian princess dead four thousand years; Jean-Marc looked at his arms: one was immobilized, with a needle slipped into the vein, the other was gesturing broadly to emphasize his words. In the past, watching him gesticulate, Jean-Marc always had the impression that in relation to his little body F.'s arms were littler still, utterly minuscule, the arms of a marionette. The impression was even stronger that day because his baby gestures were so ill suited to the gravity of his talk: F. was describing the coma that had lasted several days before the doctors brought him back to life: "You know all those accounts by people who've survived death: the tunnel with a light at the end of it. The beauty of the beyond drawing them on. Well, I swear to you, there's no light. And what's worse, no unconsciousness. You know everything, you hear everything, but they—the doctors—don't realize it, and they say everything in front of you, even things you shouldn't hear. That you're done for. That your brain is finished."

He was silent for a moment. Then: "I'm not saying my mind was completely clear. I was conscious of everything but everything was slightly distorted, like in a dream. From time to time the dream would turn into a nightmare. Only, in real life, a nightmare is over soon, you start yelling and you wake up, but I couldn't yell. And that was the worst of it: not being able to yell. Being incapable of yelling in the midst of a nightmare."

He was silent again. Then: "I never used to be

afraid of dying. Now, yes. I can't shake off the idea that after death you keep being alive. That to be dead is to live an endless nightmare. But that's enough. Enough. Let's talk about something else."

Before his arrival at the hospital, Jean-Marc had been sure that neither of them would be able to dodge the memory of their break, and that he would have to offer F. a few insincere words of reconciliation. But his fears were needless: the thought of death had made all other subjects meaningless. However much F. might want to move on to something else, he continued to talk about his suffering body. The account plunged Jean-Marc into depression but stirred no affection in him.

4

Is he really so cold, so unfeeling? One day, some years back, he learned that F. had betrayed him; ah, the term is far too romantic, certainly exaggerated; anyhow that betrayal was nothing so terrible: at a meeting held while Jean-Marc was away, everyone attacked him, and this later cost him his job (a loss that was unfortunate but not very grave, considering the meager importance he accorded his work). F. was present at that meeting. He was there and he said not a single word in Jean-Marc's defense. His tiny arms, which so loved to gesticulate, made not the slightest movement for his friend. Not wanting to be wrong, Jean-Marc took meticulous care to verify that F. really had kept silent. When he was thoroughly certain, for a few minutes he felt immensely wounded; then he decided never to see F. again; and immediately thereafter he was gripped by a sense of relief, inexplicably joyful.

F. was just finishing the report on his miseries when, after another moment of silence, his little mummified-princess face brightened: "You remember our conversations in high school?"

"Not really," said Jean-Marc.

"I would always listen to you as my authority when you talked about girls."

Jean-Marc tried to recall, but his memory yielded no trace of the long-ago conversations: "What could I have had to say about girls? I was a sixteen-year-old twerp."

"I can see myself standing there in front of you," F. went on, "saying something about girls.

You remember, it always used to shock me that a beautiful body could be a secretion machine; I told you I could hardly stand to see a girl wipe her nose. And I can see you now; you stopped, you looked at me hard, and you said in an oddly experienced tone, sincere, firm: 'Wipe her nose? For me all it takes is seeing how her eye blinks, seeing that movement of the eyelid over the cornea, and I feel a disgust I can barely control.' You remember that?"

"No," answered Jean-Marc.

"How could you forget? The movement of the eyelid. Such a strange idea!"

But Jean-Marc was telling the truth; he did not remember. Besides, he was not even trying to search his memory. He was thinking about something else: this is the real and the only reason for friendship: to provide a mirror so the other person can contemplate his image from the past, which, without the eternal blah-blah of memories between pals, would long ago have disappeared.

"The eyelid. You really don't remember that?"

"No," said Jean-Marc, and then to himself, silently: so you just won't understand that I don't give a damn about the mirror you're holding out to me?

Fatigue had come over F., who fell silent as if
the eyelid memory had exhausted him.

"You should sleep," said Jean-Marc, and he
stood up.

As he left the hospital, he felt an irresistible
yearning to be with Chantal. If he had not been
so worn out he would have left on the spot. On
his way to Brussels, he had imagined having an
elaborate breakfast the next morning and getting
on the road when he felt like it, in no rush. But
after the encounter with F., he set his travel clock
for five A.M.

5

Tired after a bad night, Chantal left the hotel.
On her way toward the shore, she kept coming
across weekend tourists. Every cluster of them
presented the same pattern: the man was pushing
a stroller with a baby in it, the woman was walking beside him; the man's expression was meek,
solicitous, smiling, a bit embarrassed, and endlessly willing to bend over the child, wipe its nose,
soothe its cries; the woman's expression was blasé,

11

distant, smug, sometimes even (inexplicably) spiteful. This pattern Chantal saw repeated in several variants: the man alongside a woman was pushing the stroller and also carrying another baby on his back, in a specially made sack; the man alongside a woman was pushing the stroller, carrying one baby on his shoulders and another in a belly carrier; the man alongside a woman had no stroller but was holding one child by the hand and carrying three others, on his back, his belly, and his shoulders. Then, finally, with no man, a woman was pushing the stroller; she was doing it with a force unseen in the men, such that Chantal, walking on the same sidewalk, had to leap out of her way at the last moment.

Chantal thinks: men have daddified themselves. They aren't fathers, they're just daddies, which means: fathers without a father's authority. She imagines trying to flirt with a daddy pushing a stroller with one baby inside it and carrying another two babies on his back and belly. Taking advantage of a moment when the wife stopped at a shop window, she would whisper an invitation to the husband. What would he do? Could the man transformed into a baby-tree still turn to look at a strange woman? Wouldn't the babies hanging off his back and his belly start howling about their carrier's disturbing movement? The idea strikes Chantal funny and puts her in a good mood. She thinks to herself: I live in a world where men will never turn to look at me again.

Then, along with a few morning strollers, she found herself on the seawall: the tide was out; before her the sandy plain stretched away over a kilometer. It was a long time since she had come to the Normandy coast, and she was unfamiliar with the activities in fashion there now: kites and sail-cars. The kite: a colored fabric stretched over a formidably tough frame, let loose into the wind; with the help of two lines, one in each hand, a person forces different directions on it, so that it climbs and drops, twists, emits a dreadful noise like a gigantic horsefly and, from time to time, nose first, falls into the sand like an airplane crashing. She was surprised to see that the owners were neither children nor adolescents but adults, almost all of them. And never women, always men. In fact, they were the daddies! The daddies without their children, the daddies who had managed to escape their wives! They didn't run off to mistresses, they ran off to the beach, to play!

Again the notion of a treacherous seduction struck her: she would come up behind the man holding the two lines and watching the noisy flight of his toy with his head thrown back; into his ear she would whisper an erotic invitation in the lewdest words. His reaction? She hadn't a doubt: without glancing at her, he would hiss: "Leave me alone, I'm busy!"

Ah, no, men will never turn to look at her again.

She returned to the hotel. But in the parking lot outside the lobby, she spotted Jean-Marc's car. At the desk, she learned that he had arrived at least a half-hour before. The receptionist handed her a message: "I got here early. I'm going out to look for you. J.-M."

"He's gone to look for me," Chantal murmured. "But where?"

"The gentleman said you were sure to be on the beach."

6

Walking toward the beach, Jean-Marc passed a bus stop. The only person there was a girl in jeans and a T-shirt; without much ardor but quite unmistakably, she was writhing her hips as if she were dancing. When he was very close, he saw her gaping mouth: she was yawning lengthily, insatiably; the great open hole was rocking gently atop the mechanically dancing body. Jean-Marc thought: she's dancing and she's bored.

He reached the seawall; down below, on the beach, he saw men with their heads thrown back releasing kites into the air. They were doing it with passion, and Jean-Marc recalled his old theory: there are three kinds of boredom: passive boredom: the girl dancing and yawning; active boredom: kite-lovers; and rebellious boredom: young people burning cars and smashing shop windows.

Farther along the beach, children twelve to fourteen years old, their small bodies buckling beneath big colored helmets, were clustered around some odd vehicles: on a cross formed by two metal bars are set one wheel in front and two behind; in the center is a long low box for a body to slide into and stretch out; above it rises a mast with a sail. Why are the children helmeted? It must mean the sport is dangerous. Yet, Jean-Marc thinks, it's mainly the strollers who are in danger from the vehicles driven by children; why doesn't someone offer them helmets? Because people who decline organized leisure activities are deserters from the great common struggle against boredom, and they deserve neither attention nor helmets.

He went down the staircase to the beach and looked carefully along the ebbing waterline; among the distant silhouettes he strained to make out Chantal; finally he recognized her; she had just stopped to gaze at the waves, the sailboats, the clouds.

He walked past children whom an instructor was seating in the sailcars, which then started to circle slowly. Other sailcars were speeding in all directions around them. There's only the sail with its guide rope to keep the vehicle straight and dodge pedestrians by swerving aside. But can a clumsy amateur really control the sail? And is the vehicle really infallible at responding to the pilot's will?

Jean-Marc watched the sailcars, and when he saw one heading at racing-car speed for Chantal, he frowned. An old man lay in the thing like an astronaut in a rocket. Flat on his back like that, the man can't see anything ahead of him! Is

Chantal vigilant enough to keep clear? He railed against her, against her overly offhand nature, and quickened his pace.

She turned halfway around. But she cannot have seen Jean-Marc, for her demeanor was still slow, the demeanor of a woman deep in thought and walking without looking about her. He would like to shout to her to stop being so distracted, to pay attention to those idiotic cars running all over the beach. Suddenly he imagines her body crushed by the car, sprawled on the sand, she is bleeding, the car is disappearing down the beach and he sees himself dash toward her. He is so upset by the image that he really does start shouting Chantal's name, the wind is strong, the beach enormous, and no one can hear his voice, so he can give himself over to that sort of sentimental theatrics and, with tears in his eyes, shout out his anguish for her; his face clenched in a grimace of weeping, for a few seconds he is living through the horror of her death.

Then, himself astounded by that curious spasm of hysteria, he saw her, in the distance, still strolling nonchalantly, peaceable, calm, pretty, infinitely touching, and he grinned at the comedy of bereavement he'd just played out, smiled

17

about it without self-reproach, because Chantal's death has been with him ever since he began to love her; now he really did set off running, waving to her as he went. But she stopped again, again she turned to the sea, and she looked at the faraway sailboats without noticing the man flailing his hand over his head.

Finally! Turning back in his direction, she seemed to see him; overjoyed, he raised his arm again. But she paid him no mind and stopped anew to look at the long line of the sea caressing the sand. Seeing her now from the side, he realized that what he had taken to be her chignon was a bandanna knotted around her head. As he drew closer (his step suddenly much less urgent), the woman he had thought was Chantal became old, ugly, pathetically other.

7

Chantal had soon tired of looking at the beach from the seawall, and decided to go back and wait for Jean-Marc in the room. But she was so sleepy! So as not to spoil the pleasure of their reunion, she decided to get a quick cup of coffee. She changed direction and headed for a big concrete and glass pavilion that housed a restaurant, a café, a casino, and a few shops.

She entered the café; music struck her, very loud. Irritated, she moved forward between the two rows of tables. In the large, empty room, two men stared at her: one, young, leaning against the front edge of the counter, in the black outfit of a café waiter; the other older, brawny, in a T-shirt, standing at the back of the room.

Thinking to take a seat, she said to the brawny one: "Can you turn off the music?"

He took a few steps toward her: "Excuse me, I didn't catch that."

Chantal looked at his muscular, tattooed arms: a naked woman with very large breasts and with a snake twining around her body.

She repeated (reducing her demand): "The music—could you turn it down?"

The man answered: "The music? You don't like it?" and Chantal saw the younger man, now behind the counter, turn the rock up louder.

The man with the tattoo was very near her. His smile seemed malicious. She capitulated: "No, I've got nothing against your music!"

And the tattooed man: "I was sure you liked it. What will you have?"

"Nothing," Chantal said. "I just wanted to look around. You have a nice place here."

"Well then, why not stay?" says the young man in black from behind her, in a disturbingly soft voice. He has moved again: now he is positioned between the two rows of tables, in the only pathway to the door. The obsequious tone of his voice has stirred panic in her. She feels caught in a snare about to close around her any minute. She wants to act fast. To get out, she will have to go through where the young man is barring her way. Like a person hell-bent on her own ruination, she moves toward the exit. She sees before her the young man's sickly sweet smile, and she feels her heart beating. Only at the last moment does he step aside and let her pass.

8

Mistaking the physical appearance of the beloved for someone else's. How often that's happened to him! Always with the same astonishment: does that mean that the difference between her and other women is so minute? How is it possible that he cannot distinguish the form of the being he loves most, the being he considers to be beyond compare?

He opens the door to the hotel room. At last, there she is. This time, without the slightest doubt, it is she, but not looking like herself either. Her face is old, her glance strangely harsh. As if the woman he had been waving at on the beach must, now and forevermore, replace the one he loves. As if he must be punished for his inability to recognize her.

"What is it? What's happened?"

"Nothing, nothing," she says.

"What do you mean, nothing? You're completely transformed."

"I slept very badly. I had almost no sleep. I've had a bad morning."

"A bad morning? Why?"

"No reason, really no reason."

"Tell me."

"Really, no reason."

He insists. She finally says: "Men don't turn to look at me anymore."

He stares at her, unable to understand what she is saying, what she means. She is sad because men don't turn to look at her anymore? He wants to say to her: And me? What about me? Me who goes searching for you for kilometers on the beach, me who shouts your name in tears and who could chase after you the length and breadth of the planet?

He doesn't say it. Instead, slowly, his tone low, he repeats her words: "Men don't turn to look at you anymore. Is that really why you're sad?"

She flushes. She flushes as he has not seen her flush for a long time. That flush seems to betray unconfessed desires. Desires so violent that Chantal cannot resist them, and she repeats: "Yes, men, they don't turn to look at me anymore."

9

When Jean-Marc appeared at the door of the room, she had every intention of being cheerful; she meant to kiss him, but she could not; ever since her stop at the café, she had been tense, edgy, and so deeply dug into her dark mood that she feared any loving gesture she might try would come across as forced and false.

Then Jean-Marc asked her: "What's happened?" She told him she had slept badly, that she was tired, but she did not manage to convince him and he continued to question her; not knowing how to escape that love inquisition, she thought to tell him something funny; her morning walk and the men transformed into baby-trees returned to mind, and she came across the phrase still lying about in her head like a little misplaced object: "Men don't turn to look at me anymore." She resorted to that phrase to avert any serious discussion; she tried to say it as lightly as possible, but to her surprise, her voice was bitter and melancholy. She could feel that melancholy plastered across her face and knew, instantly, that it would be misinterpreted.

She saw him gaze at her, lengthily, gravely, and she had the feeling that deep inside her body that gaze was touching off a fire. The fire was spreading swiftly in her belly, rising into her chest, burning her cheeks, and she could hear Jean-Marc repeat her words: "Men don't turn to look at you anymore. Is that really why you're sad?"

She felt that she was burning like a torch and that sweat was pouring off her skin; she knew this flush gave her phrase an exaggerated importance;

he must think that by those words (ah, such innocuous words!) she had given herself away, that she had shown him secret yearnings which now had her flushing for shame; it's a misunderstanding but she cannot explain it to him, because she's been acquainted with this fiery assault for some time already; she has always refused to call it by its real name, but this time she no longer has any doubts as to what it means, and for that very reason she will not, she cannot, speak of it.

The wave of heat was a long one, and it played itself out—the height of sadism—right under Jean-Marc's eyes; she could not think how to hide, cover herself, deflect the searching gaze. Deeply disturbed, she said the same phrase again, in the hope that she could rectify what she had botched the first time around, could manage to say it lightly, like a witticism, a parody: "Yes indeed, men don't turn to look at me anymore." No use, the phrase echoed even more dolefully than before.

In Jean-Marc's eyes there suddenly flares a light she knows, which is like a rescue lantern: "And me? How can you be thinking about men not turning to look at you when I go chasing endlessly after you wherever you are?"

She feels saved because Jean-Marc's voice is

the voice of love, the voice that in these moments of disarray she had forgotten existed, the voice of love, which caresses and soothes her but for which she is not yet ready; as if that voice were coming from far off, from too far off; she would need to hear it for a good long while to be capable of believing in it.

That was why, when he tried to take her in his arms, she stiffened; she was afraid to be clasped against him; afraid that her damp body would divulge the secret. The moment was too brief and gave her no time to monitor herself; and so, before she could suppress her gesture, timidly but firmly she pushed him away.

10

That spoiled meeting which made them incapable of embracing, did it really occur? Does Chantal still remember those several seconds of misapprehension? Does she still recall the phrase that upset Jean-Marc? Barely. The episode has been forgotten like thousands of others. A couple of hours later, they're lunching at the hotel restaurant and chatting merrily about death. About death? Chantal's boss has asked her to give some thought to an advertising campaign for the Lucien Duval Funeral Homes.

"We shouldn't laugh," she says, laughing.

"What about them, are they laughing?"

"Who?"

"The people you work with. The idea itself is so obviously funny, an ad campaign for death! Your boss, that old Trotskyite! You're always saying he's intelligent."

"He's intelligent, all right. Sharp as a scalpel. He knows Marx, he knows psychoanalysis, modern poetry. He likes to tell about how in the nineteen-twenties, in Germany or somewhere, there was a movement for a poetry of the everyday. Advertising, he claims, is realizing that poetic project after the fact. It transforms the simple objects of life into poetry. Thanks to advertising, everydayness has started singing."

"What's intelligent about those platitudes?"

"His tone of cynical provocation when he says them."

"Is he laughing or not laughing when he tells you to do an ad campaign for death?"

"A smile that indicates a certain distance looks

elegant, and the more powerful you are, the more you feel an obligation to be elegant. But his distant smile has nothing to do with laughter like yours. He's highly aware of the subtle difference between them."

"How does he put up with your laughter, then?"

"Please, Jean-Marc, what do you think? I never laugh. Don't forget, I've got two different faces. I've learned to draw some pleasure from the fact, but still, having two faces isn't easy. It takes effort, it takes discipline! You have to understand that whatever I do, like it or not, I do with the intention to do well. If only so as not to lose my job. And it's very hard to be a perfectionist in your work and at the same time despise that work."

"Oh, you can do it, you're capable of it, you're brilliant," says Jean-Marc.

"Yes, I can have two faces, but I can't have them at the same time. With you, I wear the scoffing face. When I'm at the office, I wear the serious face. I get the résumés of people looking for work at our place. It's up to me to recommend them or reject them. Some of them, in their letters, express themselves in this perfectly up-to-date lingo, with all the clichés, with the jargon, with all the required optimism. I don't need to see them or talk to them to detest them. But I know that those are the ones who will do the work well, and zealously. And then there are the ones who, in other times, would certainly be going into philosophy, or art history, or teaching French literature, but these days, for want of anything better, almost out of despair, they're looking for work at our place. I know that in their hearts they feel contempt for the job they're seeking and that therefore they are my kinfolk. And I have to decide."

"And how do you decide?"

"One time I recommend the person I like, the next time the person who'll do good work. I behave half as traitor to my company, half as traitor to myself. I'm a double traitor. And that state of double treason I consider not a defeat but a triumph. Because who knows how long I'll still be able to hold on to my two faces? It's exhausting. The day will come when I'll have only one face. The worse of the two, of course. The serious one. The acquiescent one. Will you still love me then?"

"You'll never lose your two faces," says Jean-Marc.

She smiles and raises her wine glass: "Let's hope not!"

They toast, they drink, and then Jean-Marc says: "Actually, I almost envy you doing advertising for death. I don't know why, since I was very young I've always been fascinated by poems about death. I've learned lots and lots of them by heart. I can recite some, you want me to? You can use them. For instance, these lines from Baudelaire, you must know them:

O Death, old captain, it's time! Let's weigh anchor!
This land bores us, O Death! Let's cast off!"

"I know that, I know that," Chantal breaks in. "It's beautiful, but it's not for us."

"What do you mean? Your old Trotskyite loves poetry! And what better consolation for a dying person than to say to himself: this land bores us? I can imagine those words in neon over the cemetery gates. For your ads, you'd only have to change them a bit: *You're getting bored with this land. Lucien Duval, the old captain, will help you weigh anchor.*"

"But my job isn't to please the dying. They're not the ones who'll be calling for Lucien Duval's services. And the living people who are burying their dead want to enjoy life, not celebrate death. Keep this in mind: it is our religion to praise life.

29

The word 'life' is the king of words. The king-word surrounded by other grand words. The word 'adventure'! The word 'future'! And the word 'hope'! By the way, do you know the code name for the atomic bomb they dropped on Hiroshima? 'Little Boy'! That's a genius, the fellow who invented that code! They couldn't have dreamed up a better one. Little boy, kid, tyke, tot—there's no word that's more tender, more touching, more loaded with future."

"Yes, I see," says Jean-Marc, delighted. "It's life itself gliding over Hiroshima, in the figure of a little boy, releasing the golden urine of hope onto the ruins. And thus was the postwar era inaugurated." He takes up his glass: "Let's drink to it!"

11

Her son was five when she buried him. Later, during the summer vacation, her sister-in-law told her: "You're too sad. You should have another child. That's the only way you'll forget." Her sister-in-law's remark wrenched her heart. Child: an existence without a biography. A shadow rapidly fading into its successor. But she did not wish to forget her child. She stood guard over his irreplaceable individuality. Against the future she was guarding a past, the neglected and disdained past that was the poor little dead child. A week later, her husband told her: "I don't want you falling into a depression. We should have another child right away. Then you'll forget." You'll forget: he didn't even try to find another way to say it! That was the moment she decided to leave him.

It was clear to her that her husband, a fairly passive man, was speaking not for himself but for the more general interests of the family group dominated by his sister. At the time, the woman was living with her third husband and the two children born of her previous marriages; she had managed to stay on good terms with her former husbands and to regroup them around her, along with the families of her brothers and her cousins. Their huge gatherings took place in an enormous country house during school vacations; she tried to bring Chantal into the tribe so that bit by bit, imperceptibly, she would become part of it.

There, in that big house, first her sister-in-law and then her husband exhorted her to have another child. And there, in a little bedroom, she refused to make love with him. Every one of his erotic invitations reminded her of the family campaign for another pregnancy, and the idea of making love with him became grotesque. She felt as if all the members of the tribe—grandmothers, daddies, nephews, nieces, cousins—were eaves-dropping on them from behind the door, were secretly inspecting their bedsheets, evaluating their morning fatigue. They all assumed rights of scrutiny over her belly. Even the little nephews were enlisted as mercenaries in the war. One of them asked her: "Chantal, why don't you like children?" "Why do you think I don't like chil-dren?" she responded curtly and coldly. He did-n't know what to say. Irritated, she went on: "Who told you I don't like children?" And the lit-tle nephew, beneath her severe gaze, answered in a tone that was at once timid and assured: "If you liked children you could have some."

When she returned from that vacation, she moved decisively: first she determined to go back to work. Before her son was born, she had taught high school. Since the work was poorly paid, she decided against resuming it and chose instead a profession that she liked less (she loved teaching) but that paid three times as much. She felt guilty at betraying her own inclinations for the sake of money, but this was the only way to obtain her independence. To obtain it, nevertheless, money wasn't enough. She also needed a man, a man who would be the living example of a different life, because though she yearned desperately to escape her earlier life, she could not imagine another.

She was to wait a few years before meeting Jean-Marc. Two weeks after that, she asked her astonished husband for a divorce. Her sister-in-law, admiration mixed with hostility, called her the Tigress: "You're stock-still, nobody knows what you're thinking, and then you pounce." Three months later she bought an apartment and, dismissing any notion of marriage, moved into it with the man she loved.

12

Jean-Marc had a dream: he is worried about Chantal, he is looking for her, running through the streets, and finally he sees her from behind, walking off. He runs after her and shouts her name. He is no more than a few steps away, she turns her head, and Jean-Marc is transfixed by the different face before him, an alien and disagreeable face. Yet it is not someone different, it is Chantal, his Chantal, he has no doubt of that, but his Chantal with a stranger's face, and this is horrifying, this is unbearably horrifying. He grasps her, holds her to his body, and, sobbing, he chants: "Chantal, my little Chantal, my little Chantal," as if he hoped by repeating the words to infuse this transformed face with its old, vanished look, its vanished identity.

The dream woke him. Chantal was no longer in bed, he heard the morning sounds from the bathroom. Still in the grip of the dream, he felt an urgent need to see her. He rose and went toward the half-open door of the bathroom. There he stopped, and like a voyeur avid to steal a glimpse of some intimate scene, he watched her: yes, it was his Chantal as he had always known her: she was leaning over the basin, brushing her teeth and spitting out her saliva mingled with toothpaste, and she was so comically, so childishly focused on her activity that Jean-Marc grinned. Then, as if she felt his gaze, she pivoted about, saw him in the doorway, flared up, and ultimately let herself be kissed on her still quite white mouth.

"Will you pick me up at the agency tonight?" she asked him.

At about six he came into the lobby, turned down the corridor, and stopped at her door. It was ajar, as the bathroom door had been in the morning. Chantal was in her office with two women, her colleagues. But this was no longer the same woman as that morning; she was talking in a louder voice than he was used to from her, and her gestures were quicker, brusquer, more imperious. That morning, in the bathroom, he had recovered the being he'd lost during the night, and now, in the late afternoon, she was changing again before his eyes.

He went in. She smiled at him. But the smile was fixed, and Chantal almost rigid. In France, over the past twenty years, kissing on both cheeks has become an almost obligatory convention and, for that reason, painful for people who love each other. But how can they avoid the convention when they meet where others see them and they don't wish to seem a couple at odds? Self-conscious, Chantal approached and offered him both her cheeks. The gesture was artificial, and it left them with a false taste. They went out, and only after a while did he see her again as the Chantal he had known.

It is always that way: between the moment he meets her again and the moment he recognizes her for the woman he loves, he has some distance to go. At their first encounter, in the mountains, he had had the luck to get away alone with her almost immediately. If, before that one-on-one encounter, he had spent much time with her as she was among other people, would he have recognized her as the beloved being? If he had known her only with the face she shows her colleagues, her bosses, her subordinates, would that face have moved and enchanted him? To these questions he has no answer.

13

Maybe his hypersensitivity to such moments of alienation was the reason the phrase "men don't turn to look at me anymore" affected him so powerfully: saying it, Chantal was barely recognizable. That phrase was unlike her. And her face, looking harsh, looking old, was unlike her too. His first reaction was jealousy: how could she complain that men had lost interest in her when, that very morning, he had been willing to get himself killed on the highway for the sake of being with her as soon as possible? But less than an hour later, he came around to thinking: every woman measures how much she's aged by the interest or uninterest men show in her body. Wouldn't it be ridiculous to take offense at that? Still, without taking offense, he did not agree. Because on the day they first met he had already noted traces of slight aging on her face (she is older than he by four years). Her beauty, which struck him at the time, did not make her look younger than her age; he might sooner have said that her age made her beauty more eloquent.

Chantal's phrase echoed in his head and he imagined the story of her body: it was lost among millions of other bodies until the day a look of desire settled on it and drew it forth from the nebulous multitude; then the number of such looks increased and set afire this body, which ever since has been moving through the world like a torch; now is its time of radiant glory, but soon the looks will start to grow fewer, the light to dim little by little, until the day when this translucent, then transparent, then invisible body will pace the streets like a small itinerant non-being. On this journey from the first invisibility to the second, the phrase "men don't turn to look at me anymore" is the red light signaling that the body's gradual extinction has begun.

However much he may tell her he loves her and thinks her beautiful, his loving gaze could never console her. Because the gaze of love is the gaze that isolates. Jean-Marc thought about the loving solitude of two old persons become invisible to other people: a sad solitude that prefigures death. No, what she needs is not a loving gaze but a flood of alien, crude, lustful looks settling on her with no good will, no discrimination, no tenderness or politeness—settling on her fatefully, inescapably. Those are the looks that sustain her within human society. The gaze of love rips her out of it.

With some remorse he recalled the dizzyingly headlong beginnings of their love. He did not have to conquer her: she was conquered from the first instant. Turn to look at her? No need. She was instantly with him, in front of him, beside him. From the start, he was the stronger one and she the weaker. This inequality was laid into the foundations of their love. Unjustifiable inequality, iniquitous inequality. She was weaker because she was older.

14

When she was sixteen, seventeen years old, she used to cherish a certain metaphor; had she invented it herself, heard it, read it? no matter: she wanted to be a rose fragrance, a pervasive, overwhelming fragrance, she wanted to move thus through all men and, by way of the men, to embrace the entire world. The pervasive rose fragrance: a metaphor of adventure. At the threshold of her adult life, that metaphor unfolded like the romantic promise of a sweet promiscuity, like an invitation to the journey through men. But she was not by nature a woman born to run through lovers, and this vague, lyrical dream quickly fell dormant in her marriage, which started off calm and happy.

Much later, after she had left her husband and lived several years with Jean-Marc, she was at the seashore one day: they were dining outdoors, on a wooden deck over the water; she retains an intense memory of whiteness: the deck, the tables, the chairs, the tablecloths, everything was white, the lampposts were painted white and the bulbs beamed a white light against the summer sky, not yet dark, where the moon, itself white too, was whitening everything around them. And in this bath of white she was struck by a feeling of unbearable nostalgia for Jean-Marc.

Nostalgia? How could she feel nostalgia when he was right in front of her? How can you suffer from the absence of a person who is present? (Jean-Marc knew how to answer that: you can suffer nostalgia in the presence of the beloved if you glimpse a future where the beloved is no more; if the beloved's death is, invisibly, already present.)

During that moment of strange nostalgia at the seaside, she suddenly thought of her dead child, and a wave of happiness flooded over her. Soon she would be frightened by this feeling. But no one can do a thing about feelings, they exist and there's no way to censor them. We can reproach ourselves for some action, for a remark, but not for a feeling, quite simply because we have no control at all over it. The memory of her dead son filled her with happiness and she could only ask herself what that meant. The answer was clear: it meant that her presence at Jean-Marc's side was absolute and that the reason it could be absolute was the absence of her son. She was happy that her son was dead. Seated across from Jean-Marc, she wished she could say this aloud but did not dare. She was not confident of his reaction, she feared he would see her as a monster.

She relished the utter absence of adventures. Adventure: a means of embracing the world. She no longer wanted to embrace the world. She no longer wanted the world. She relished the happiness of being adventureless and without desire for adventures. She recalled her metaphor and saw a rose withering, rapidly as in a time-lapse film until all that was left of it was a skinny blackish twig, and disappearing forever in the white universe of their evening: the rose diluted in the whiteness.

That same evening, just before falling asleep (Jean-Marc was sleeping already), again she remembered her dead child and the memory was again accompanied by that scandalous wave of happiness. She realized then that her love for

Jean-Marc was a heresy, a transgression of the unwritten laws of the human community from which she was drawing apart; she realized she would have to keep secret the exorbitance of her love to avoid stirring up people's malevolent fury.

15

Mornings, she is always the one to leave the apartment first and the one to open the mailbox, leaving the letters addressed to Jean-Marc and taking her own. That morning, she found two letters: one to Jean-Marc (she glanced furtively at it: the postmark was Brussels), the other to her, but without an address or a stamp. Someone must have brought it personally. She was a little rushed, so she put it unopened into her purse and hurried toward the bus. Once she was seated, she opened the envelope; the letter contained only one sentence: "I follow you around like a spy—you are beautiful, very beautiful."

Her first reaction was unpleasant. Without asking her permission, someone was trying to intrude in her life, draw her attention (her capacity for attention is limited and she hasn't the energy to expand it), in short, to bother her. Then she told herself that after all it was unimportant. What woman hasn't gotten such a message sometime or other? She reread the letter and realized that the woman seated beside her could read it too. She put it back into her purse and glanced around her. She saw people in their seats gazing distractedly out the window at the street, two girls exaggerating a laughing fit, near the exit a young black man, tall and handsome, staring at her, and a woman deep in a book who probably had a long trip ahead of her.

Usually, on the bus, she would ignore everyone else. This time, though, because of that letter, she believed herself watched, and she watched too. Was there always someone staring at her, the way the black man was today? As if he knew what she had just read, he smiled at her. What if he were the one who wrote the message? She quickly rejected that idea as too absurd and rose to get off at the next stop. She would have to slip past the black man, who was blocking the way to the exit, and that made her uncomfortable. When she was right near him, the bus braked, for an instant she lost her balance, and the black man, who was still staring at her, guffawed. She left the bus and said to herself: that wasn't flirting, that was mockery.

She kept hearing that mocking laughter all day long, like a bad omen. She looked at the letter two or three times again in her office, and back at home later, she considered what to do about it. Keep it? What for? Show it to Jean-Marc? That would embarrass her, as if she'd meant to boast! Well then, destroy it? Of course. She went into the bathroom, and leaning over the toilet, she looked at the liquid surface; she tore the envelope into several bits, threw them in, flushed, but the letter she refolded and carried into her bedroom. She opened the wardrobe and put the letter underneath her brassieres. As she did this, she heard the black man's mocking laughter again and thought that she was just like every other woman; her brassieres suddenly looked vulgar and idiotically feminine.

16

Scarcely an hour later, coming into the house, Jean-Marc showed Chantal an announcement: "I found it in the mailbox this morning. F. died."

Chantal was almost pleased that another letter, a more serious one, should overshadow the silliness of hers. She took Jean-Marc by the arm and drew him into the living room where she sat down facing him.

Chantal: "You're upset after all."

"No," said Jean-Marc, "or rather, I'm upset that I'm not."

"And even now you haven't forgiven him?"

"I've forgiven him everything. But that's not the point. I told you about that strange feeling of joy I had when I decided, back then, not to see him anymore. I was cold as an ice cube and that pleased me. Well, his death hasn't changed that feeling at all."

"You frighten me. You really do frighten me."

Jean-Marc rose to get the bottle of cognac and two glasses. Then, after swallowing a mouthful: "At the end of my hospital visit, he began to reminisce. He reminded me what I must have said when I was sixteen. When he did that, I understood the sole meaning of friendship as it's practiced today. Friendship is indispensable to man for the proper function of his memory. Remembering our past, carrying it with us always, may be the necessary requirement for maintaining, as they say, the wholeness of the self. To ensure that the self doesn't shrink, to see that it holds on to its volume, memories have to be watered like potted flowers, and the watering calls for regular contact with the witnesses of the past, that is to say, with friends. They are our mirror; our memory; we ask nothing of them but that they polish the mirror from time to time so we can look at ourselves in it. But I don't care a damn about what I did in high school! What I've always wanted, since my early adolescence, maybe even since childhood, was something else entirely: friendship as a value prized above all others. I liked to say: between the truth and a friend, I always choose the friend. I said it to be provocative, but I really thought it. Today I know that maxim is obsolete. It might have been valid for Achilles as Patroclus' friend, for Alexandre Dumas' musketeers, even for Sancho Panza, who was a true friend to his master despite all their disagreements. But for us it isn't anymore. I've gotten so pessimistic that these days I'd even choose the truth over friendship."

He took another swallow: "Friendship, to me, was proof of the existence of something stronger than ideology, than religion, than the nation. In

Dumas' book, the four friends often find themselves on opposite sides and thus required to fight against one another. But that doesn't affect their friendship. They still go on helping one another, secretly, cunningly, without giving a damn for the truths of their respective camps. They put their friendship above the truth, or the cause, or orders from superiors, above the king, above the queen, above everything."

Chantal caressed his hand, and after a pause he went on: "Dumas wrote the story of the musketeers two hundred years after their time. Was he already feeling nostalgia then for the lost universe of friendship? Or is the disappearance of friendship a more recent phenomenon?"

"I can't answer that. Friendship isn't a problem for women."

"What do you mean?"

"Just what I say. Friendship is a problem for men. It's their romanticism. Not ours."

Jean-Marc fell silent, swallowed a mouthful of cognac, and came back to his thought: "How is friendship born? Certainly as an alliance against adversity, an alliance without which man would be helpless before his enemies. Maybe there's no longer a vital need for such an alliance."

47

"There will always be enemies."

"Yes, but they're invisible and anonymous. Bureaucracies, laws. What can a friend do for you when they decide to build an airport outside your windows, or when they fire you? If anyone helps you, again it's somebody anonymous, invisible, a social-service outfit, a consumer watchdog organization, a law firm. Friendship can no longer be proved by some exploit. The occasion no longer lends itself to searching out your wounded friend on the battlefield or unsheathing your saber to defend him against bandits. We go through our lives without great perils, but also without friendship."

"If that's true, that should have brought you to reconcile with F."

"I freely acknowledge that he would not have understood my reproaches if I'd made them known to him. When the other people jumped on me, he kept quiet. But I have to be fair: he considered his silence to be courageous. Someone told me he even boasted of not knuckling under to the prevailing psychosis about me and of not having said anything that could hurt me. So his conscience was clear, and he must have felt wounded when, inexplicably, I stopped seeing him. I was wrong to hope for more from him than neutrality. If he had put himself on the line to defend me in that bitter, spiteful world, he would have risked disgrace, conflicts, trouble for himself. How could I demand that of him? Especially since he was my friend! That would have been extremely unfriendlike of me! To put it another way: it was impolite. Because friendship emptied of its traditional content is transformed these days into a contract of mutual consideration, in short, a contract of politeness. Well, it's impolite to ask a friend for something that could be embarrassing or unpleasant for him."

"Well, yes, that's how things are. All the more reason why you should say it without bitterness. Without irony."

"I'm saying it without irony. That's how things are."

"If hatred strikes you, if you get accused, thrown to the lions, you can expect one of two reactions from people who know you: some of them will join in the kill, the others will very discreetly pretend to know nothing, hear nothing, so you can go right on seeing them and talking to them. That second category, discreet and tactful, those are your friends. 'Friends' in the modern

sense of the term. Listen, Jean-Marc, I've known
that forever."

17

On the screen is a behind in horizontal position, good-looking, sexy, in close-up. A hand is
caressing it tenderly, enjoying the skin of this
naked, compliant body. Then the camera pulls
back and we see the body entire, lying on a small
bed: it is a baby, with its mother leaning over it.
In the next sequence she lifts him up and her
parted lips kiss the lax, wet, wide-open mouth of
the nursling. At that instant the camera draws in,
and the same kiss, by itself, in close-up, suddenly
becomes a sensual love kiss.

There Leroy stopped the film: "We're always
looking for a majority. Like the candidates for
president in an American election campaign. We
set a product within the magic circle of a few
images likely to attract a majority of buyers. In
the search for those images, we tend to overvalue
sexuality. I want to alert you. Only a very small
minority really enjoys sex."

Leroy paused a moment to savor the surprise of the little gathering of colleagues he called in once a week for a seminar around a campaign, a television spot, a billboard. They had long been aware that what flattered their boss was not their quick acquiescence but their astonishment. For that reason, a refined lady, with many rings on her aged fingers, dared to contradict him: "All the polls say the opposite!"

"Of course they do," said Leroy. "If someone interrogates you, my dear lady, on your sex life, are you going to tell the truth? Even if the person doesn't know your name, even if he's asking his questions over the phone and doesn't see you, you're going to lie: 'Do you like to fuck?' 'And how!' 'How often?' 'Six times a day!' 'Do you like dirty sex?' 'Crazy about it!' But all that is hogwash. When it comes to commerce, the erotic is a touchy issue, because while everyone may covet the erotic life, everyone also hates it, as the source of their troubles, their frustrations, their yearnings, their complexes, their sufferings."

Again he showed them that sequence in the television spot; Chantal watches the wet lips touching the other wet lips in close-up, and she realizes (it's the first time she realizes it so clearly) that Jean-Marc and she never kiss that way. She herself is amazed: is this true? have they really never kissed like that?

Yes, they have. It was back when they still didn't know each other by name. In the great hall of a mountain lodge, with people drinking and chattering around them, they exchanged a few commonplaces, but the tone of their voices made it clear that they wanted each other, and they withdrew into an empty corridor where, wordlessly, they kissed. She opened her mouth and pressed her tongue into Jean-Marc's mouth, eager to lick whatever she would find inside. This zeal of their tongues was not a sensual necessity but an urgency to let each other know that they were prepared to make love, right away, instantly, fully and wildly and without losing a moment. Their two salivas had nothing to do with desire or pleasure, they were messengers. Neither person had the courage to say outright and aloud, "I want to make love with you, right now, without delay," so they let their salivas speak for them. That is why, during their lovemaking (which followed their first kiss by a few hours), their mouths probably (she no longer remembers, but as time goes on she's nearly certain) held no further interest for each other, did not touch, did not lick, and did not even register that scandalous mutual uninterest.

Again Leroy stopped the spot: "The issue is to find the images that keep up the erotic appeal without intensifying the frustrations. That's what interests us in this sequence: the sensual imagination is titillated, but then it's immediately deflected into the maternal realm. Because intimate bodily contact, the absence of personal secrecy, the blending of salivas aren't exclusively the property of adult eroticism, they all also occur in the connection between baby and mother, the connection that is the original paradise of all physical pleasures. Incidentally, somebody's filmed the life of a fetus inside a mama-to-be. In an acrobatic contortion that we could never imitate for ourselves, the fetus was fellating its own tiny organ. You see, sexuality is not the exclusive property of young, well-built bodies that rouse bitter envy. The fetus's self-fellation will move every grandmother in the world, even the sourest ones, even the most prudish. Because the baby is the strongest, the broadest, the most reliable common denominator of all majorities. And a fetus, my dear friends, is more than a baby—it's an arch-baby, a superbaby!"

And again he had them look at the spot, and again Chantal experienced a slight repugnance at the sight of two wet mouths touching. She recalled hearing that in China and Japan the erotic culture has no open-mouth kiss. The exchange of salivas is thus not an inevitable element of eroticism but a caprice, a deviation, a specifically Western dirtiness.

The screening done, Leroy wound up: "Mommy's saliva—that's the glue that will bind the majority we mean to draw together and make into customers of the Roubachoff brand." And Chantal revises her old metaphor: it is not an immaterial, poetic rose fragrance that passes through men but material, prosaic salivas, which move with their army of microbes from the mistress's mouth to her lover's, from the lover to his wife, from the wife to her baby, from the baby to its aunt, from the aunt—a waitress—to the customer whose soup she's spat in, from the customer to his wife, from the wife to her lover, and from there to other mouths and to others still, so that every one of us is immersed in a sea of salivas that blend and make us into one single community of salivas, one humankind wet and bound together.

18

That evening, amid the noise of engines and horns, she went home exhausted. Eager for silence, she opened the apartment-house door and heard hammering and the shouts of workmen. The elevator was out of order. Climbing the stairs, she felt the detestable wave of heat invade her, and the hammer blows echoing throughout the elevator shaft were like a drumroll for that heat, heightening and amplifying and glorifying it. Wet with sweat, she stopped outside the apartment door and waited a minute so Jean-Marc would not see her in that red disguise.

"The crematory fire is leaving me its visiting card," she thought. The line was not her own invention; it crossed her mind without her knowing how. Standing before the door, in the ceaseless racket, she repeated it several times to herself. She did not like the line, whose ostentatiously macabre style struck her as poor taste, but she could not shake it off.

The hammers finally fell silent, the heat began to subside, and she went in. Jean-Marc kissed her, but as he was telling her some story, the hammering began again, though the slightest bit quieter. She felt hunted, unable to hide anywhere. Her skin still damp, she said with no logical connection: "The crematory fire is the only way not to leave our bodies to their mercy."

She saw Jean-Marc's startled look and realized the oddity of what she'd just said; quickly she began talking about the television spot she had seen and what Leroy had told them, especially about the fetus photographed inside the maternal belly. Who in his acrobatic position performed a kind of masturbation so perfect that no adult could match it.

"A fetus with a sex life, imagine! It has no consciousness yet, no individuality, no perception of anything, but it already feels a sexual impulse and maybe even pleasure. So our sexuality precedes our self-awareness. Our self doesn't yet exist, but our lust is already there. And, imagine, all my colleagues found this idea touching! They had tears in their eyes over the masturbating fetus!"

"What about you?"

"Oh, what I felt was revulsion. Ah, Jean-Marc, revulsion."

Strangely moved, she took him in her arms,

clutched him against her, and stayed that way for several long moments.

Then she went on: "You realize that even in your mother's belly, which they call sacred, you're not out of reach. They film you, they spy on you, they observe your masturbation. Your poor little fetus-masturbation. You'll never escape them while you're living, everybody knows that. But you don't even escape them before you're born. Just as you won't escape them after you die. I remember something I read in the papers once: a person living in exile under a grand Russian aristocratic name was suspected of being an impostor. After he died, to thwart his claim to nobility, they dug up the long-buried remains of a peasant woman who they said was his mother. They dissected her bones, analyzed her genes. I'd like to know what lofty cause gave them the right to dig her up, the poor woman! To rifle her naked-ness, that absolute nakedness, the supranakedness of the skeleton! Ah, Jean-Marc, all I feel is revul-sion, nothing but revulsion. And do you know the story about Haydn's head? They cut it away from the still-warm cadaver so some insane scientist could take apart the brain and pinpoint the loca-tion of musical genius. And the Einstein story?

He'd carefully written his will with instructions to cremate him. They followed his orders, but his disciple, ever loyal and devoted, refused to live without the master's gaze on him. Before the cremation, he took the eyes out of the cadaver and put them in a bottle of alcohol to keep them watching him until the moment he should die himself. That's why I just said that the crematory fire is the only way our bodies can escape them. It's the only absolute death. And I don't want any other. Jean-Marc, I want an absolute death."

After a pause, the hammer blows resonated again in the room.

"Cremated, I'd be sure never to hear them again."

"Chantal, what's got into you?"

She looked at him, then turned her back, moved once more. Moved, this time, not by what she had just said but by Jean-Marc's voice, heavy with concern for her.

19

The folllowing day, she went to the cemetery (as she did at least once a month) and stood at her son's grave. When she is there, she always talks with him, and today, as if she needed to explain or excuse herself, she told him, "Darling, my darling, don't think I don't love you or that I didn't love you, but it's precisely because I loved you that I couldn't have become what I am today if you were still here. It's impossible to have a child and despise the world as it is, because that's the world we've put the child into. The child makes us care about the world, think about its future, willingly join in its racket and its turmoils, take its incurable stupidity seriously. By your death you deprived me of the pleasure of being with you, but at the same time you set me free. Free in my confrontation with the world I don't like. And the reason I can allow myself to dislike it is that you're no longer here. My dark thoughts can't bring any curse down on you. I want to tell you now, all these years after you left me, that I've come to understand your death as a gift and that I've finally accepted that dreadful gift."

20

The next morning, she found in the box an envelope with the same unknown handwriting on it. The letter hadn't the earlier laconic lightness. It read like a lengthy legal deposition. "Last Saturday," her correspondent writes, "it was nine twenty-five in the morning, you left your house earlier than other days. I usually follow you on your trip to the bus stop, but this time you walked the opposite way. You were carrying a valise and you went into a dry cleaner's. The woman there apparently knows you and perhaps likes you. I watched her from outside: her face brightened as if she'd wakened from a doze, you must have made some joke, I heard her laugh, a laugh you'd provoked and in which I thought I could make out a reflection of your face. Then you left, with your valise full. Full of your sweaters, or of tablecloths, or bed linens? Anyhow, your valise looked to me like something artificially added on to your life." He describes her dress and the beads around her neck. "I'd never seen those beads before. They are beautiful. Their red becomes you. It lights you up."

This time the letter is signed: C.D.B. That intrigues her. The first one had no signature, and she could think that its anonymity was, so to speak, sincere. Some unknown person saluting her and then immediately vanishing. But a signature, even abbreviated, indicates an intention to make oneself known, step by step, slowly but inevitably. C.D.B., she repeats to herself, smiling: Cyrille-Didier Bourguiba. Charles-David Barberousse.

She ponders the text: this man must have followed her in the street; "I follow you around like a spy," he had written in the first letter; so she should have seen him. But she observes the world around her with very little interest, and did even less that day, since Jean-Marc was with her. And besides, it was he and not she who had made the dry-cleaning woman laugh and who was carrying the valise. She reads those words again: "your valise looked to me like something artificially added on to your life." How was the valise "added on" to her life if it wasn't Chantal carrying it? The thing "added on" to her life—isn't that Jean-Marc himself? Was her correspondent trying, in an oblique way, to attack her beloved? Then, with amusement, she recognizes the comical nature of her reaction: she is capable of standing up for Jean-Marc even against an imaginary lover.

Like the first time, she did not know what to do with the letter, and the ballet of hesitation played itself out again in all its phases: she contemplated the toilet bowl, where she prepared to throw it; she tore the envelope into small bits and flushed them down; she then folded the letter itself, carried it into her room, and slipped it under her brassieres. Leaning into the lingerie shelves, she heard the door open. She quickly closed the wardrobe and turned around: Jean-Marc is on the doorsill.

He moves slowly toward her and looks at her as never before, his gaze unpleasantly focused, and when he is very close he takes her by the elbows, and holding her a step or so in front of him, he goes on looking at her. She is flustered by this, unable to say a thing. When her discomfiture becomes unbearable, he clasps her to him and says, laughing: "I wanted to see your eyelid washing your cornea like a wiper washing a windshield."

21

Since his last encounter with F., he has been thinking about it: the eye: the window to the soul; the center of the face's beauty; the point where a person's identity is concentrated; but at the same time an optical instrument that requires constant washing, wetting, maintenance by a special liquid dosed with salt. So the gaze, the greatest marvel man possesses, is regularly interrupted by a mechanical washing action. Like a windshield washed by a wiper. And nowadays you can even set the tempo of the windshield wiper in such a way that the movements are separated by a ten-second pause, which is, roughly, an eyelid's rhythm.

Jean-Marc watches the eyes of people he talks to and tries to observe the action of the eyelid; he finds that it is not easy. We are not accustomed to be aware of the eyelid. He thinks: there's nothing I see so often as other people's eyes, thus the eyelids and their movements. And yet I don't register that movement. I delete it from the eyes in front of me.

And he goes on thinking: puttering in His workshop, God stumbled onto this body form to which we must each become the soul for a short while. But what a sorry fate, to be the soul of a body cobbled together so offhandedly, whose eye cannot do its looking without being washed every ten, twenty seconds! How are we to believe that the person we see before us is a free, independent being, his own master? How are we to believe that his body is the faithful expression of whatever soul inhabits it? To be able to believe that, we've had to forget about the perpetual blinking of the eyelid. We've had to forget the putterer's workshop we come from. We've had to submit to a contract to forget. It's God Himself who imposed the contract on us.

But between Jean-Marc's childhood and his adolescence, there certainly must have been a brief period when he wasn't yet acquainted with that commitment to forget and when, dumbfounded, he would watch the eyelid slide across the eye: he saw that the eye is not a window that shows the unique and miraculous soul, but a jerry-built mechanism that someone set in motion back in time immemorial. This moment of sudden adolescent insight must have been a shock. "You stopped," F. had told him, "you looked at me hard, and you said, in an oddly firm tone: 'For

me all it takes is seeing how her eye blinks. . . .'"
Jean-Marc had no recollection of it. It was a
shock destined to be forgotten. And, indeed, he
would have forgotten it for good if F. had not
reminded him of it.

Deep in thought, he returned to the apartment
and opened the door to Chantal's room. She was
putting something away in her wardrobe, and
Jean-Marc wanted to see her eyelid wipe her eye,
her eye that to him is the window to an ineffable
soul. He went to her, grasped her by the elbows,
and looked into her eyes; indeed, they were blinking, rather fast, even, as if she knew she was
being examined.

He saw the eyelid drop and rise, fast, too fast,
and he wanted to reexperience his own sensation,
the sensation of the sixteen-year-old Jean-Marc
who found the ocular mechanism desperately dis-
appointing. But the abnormal tempo of the eyelid and the sudden irregularity of its movements
touched him more than they disappointed him:
he saw the windshield wiper of Chantal's eyelid
as her soul's wing, a wing that trembled, that
panicked, that fluttered. The feeling was sudden
as a lightning flash, and he clutched Chantal to
him.

Then he relaxed his grip and saw her face, flustered, frightened. He told her: "I wanted to see your eyelid washing your cornea like a wiper washing a windshield."

"I have no idea what you're talking about," she said, her tension suddenly gone.

And he told her about the forgotten memory his unloved friend had called up.

22

"When F. reminded me of the remark I must have made in high school, I felt I was hearing something completely absurd."

"No, not at all," Chantal answered. "As the person I know, you certainly must have said it. It all fits. Remember when you were studying medicine?"

He never underestimated the magic a man feels about the moment he chooses his career. Fully aware that life is too short for the choice to be anything but irreparable, he had been distressed to discover that he felt no spontaneous attraction to any occupation. Rather skeptically, he looked over the array of available possibilities: prosecutors, who spend their whole lives persecuting people; schoolteachers, the butt of rowdy children; science and technology, whose advances bring enormous harm along with a small benefit; the sophisticated, empty chatter of the social sciences; interior design (which appealed to him because of his memories of his cabinetmaker grandfather), utterly enslaved by fashions he detested; the occupation of the poor pharmacists, now reduced to peddlers of boxes and bottles. When he wondered: what should I choose for my whole life's work? his inner self would fall into the most uncomfortable silence. When finally he decided on medicine, he was responding not to some secret predilection but rather to an altruistic idealism: he considered medicine the only occupation incontestably useful to man, and one whose technological advances entail the fewest negative effects.

The letdown was not long in coming, when in the course of the second year he had to do his stint in the dissection room: he suffered a shock from which he never recovered: he was incapable of looking squarely at death; shortly thereafter he acknowledged that the truth was even worse: he was incapable of looking squarely at a body:

its inescapable, unresponding imperfection; the decomposition clock that governs its functioning; its blood, its guts, its pain.

When he told F. of his disgust at the eyelid's movement, he must have been sixteen. When he decided to study medicine, he must have been nineteen; by then, having already signed on to the contract to forget, he no longer remembered what he had said to F. three years before. Too bad for him. The memory might have alerted him. It might have helped him see that his choice of medicine was wholly theoretical, made without the slightest self-knowledge.

Thus he studied medicine for three years before giving up with a sense of shipwreck. What to choose after those lost years? What to attach to, if his inner self should keep as silent as it had before? He walked down the broad outside staircase of the medical school for the last time, with the feeling that he was about to find himself alone on a platform all the trains had left.

23

In an effort to identify her correspondent, Chantal discreetly but carefully looks about her. At the corner of their street is a bistro: the ideal spot for anyone who should want to spy on her; from there one could see the door to her apartment house, the two streets she walked along every day, and her bus stop. She went in, sat down, ordered a coffee, and inspected the customers. At the counter she saw a young man who looked away when she entered. He was a regular customer, whom she knew by sight. She even remembered that in the past their eyes had often met and that later on he pretended not to see her.

Another day, she pointed him out to the woman from next door. "Sure, that's Monsieur Dubarreau!" "Dubarreau or du Barreau?" The neighbor didn't know. "What about his first name? Do you know that?" No, she didn't.

Du Barreau, that would fit. In that case her admirer isn't some Charles-Didier or Christophe-David, the initial "D" would stand for the particle "du," and du Barreau would have only one first name. Cyrille du Barreau. Or better: Charles.

She imagines a family of penniless aristocrats from the provinces. Family comically proud of its particle. She pictures Charles du Barreau standing at the counter, making a show of his indifference, and she says to herself that the particle suits him, that it goes perfectly with his blasé manner.

Soon after, she is walking in the street with Jean-Marc, and du Barreau comes toward them. She has the red beads around her neck. They were a gift from Jean-Marc, but considering them too showy, she wore them only rarely. She realizes that she has put them on because du Barreau considered them beautiful. He must think (and with good reason, in fact!) that it is for his sake, for him, that she is wearing them. Briefly he looks at her, she looks at him too, and thinking of the beads, she flushes. She flushes down to her breasts, and she is sure he must have noticed. But they have already passed him, he is already far beyond them, and it is Jean-Marc who is astonished: "You're flushing! How come? What's happening?"

She is astonished too; why did she flush? Out of shame at granting this man too much attention? But the attention she's granting him is no more than trivial curiosity! Good Lord, why does she flush so often lately, so easily, like an adolescent?

As an adolescent, it's true, she did flush a lot; she was at the start of a woman's physiological journey, and her body was turning into a burdensome thing she was ashamed of. As an adult, she forgot about flushing. Then the gusts of heat heralded the end of that journey, and once again her body shamed her. With her sense of shame reawakened, she relearned to flush.

24

More letters arrived, and she was less and less able to ignore them. They were intelligent, decent, with nothing ridiculous about them, nothing importunate. Her correspondent wanted nothing, asked nothing, insisted on nothing. He was wise enough (or canny enough) to leave undescribed his own personality, his life, his feelings, his desires. He was a spy; he wrote only about her. These were letters not of seduction but of admiration. And if seduction was at all present in them, it was conceived as a long-term project. The most recent letter, though, was bolder: "For three days, I lost sight of you. When I saw you again, I marveled at your bearing, so light, so thirsty for the heights. You were like flames that must dance and leap to exist at all. More long-limbed than ever, you were striding along surrounded by bright, bacchic, drunken, wild flames. Thinking of you, I fling a mantle stitched of flame over your naked body. I swathe your white body in a cardinal's crimson mantle. And then I put you, draped like that, into a red room on a red bed, my red cardinal, most gorgeous cardinal!"

A few days later, she bought a red nightgown. She was at home, looking at herself in the mirror. She gazed at herself from every angle, slowly lifted the hem of the gown and felt she had never been so long of limb, never had skin so white.

Jean-Marc arrived. He was surprised to see Chantal, with her alluring step and her magnificent red nightgown, walk toward him, circle him, elude him, let him come near only to flee him again. Letting himself be seduced by the game, he pursued her throughout the apartment. Suddenly it is the immemorial situation of a woman being chased down by a man, and it fascinates him. She darts about the great round table, herself intoxicated by the image of a woman running from a man who desires her, then she rushes to the bed and bundles her gown up to her neck. That day he makes love to her with a new, unexpected force, and suddenly she has the sense that someone is there in the room observing them with an insane concentration, she sees his face, the face of Charles du Barreau, who imposed the red gown on her, who imposed this act of love on her, and picturing him, she cries out in climax.

Now they lie breathing side by side, and the image of her spy arouses her; in Jean-Marc's ear she whispers about slipping the crimson mantle over her naked body and walking like a gorgeous cardinal through a crowded church. At these words, he takes her in his arms again and, rocking on the waves of fantasies she keeps telling him, he again makes love to her.

Then all grows calm; before her eyes she sees only her red gown, rumpled by their bodies, at a corner of the bed. Before her half-closed eyes, that red patch turns into a rose garden, and she smells the faint fragrance nearly forgotten, the fragrance of the rose yearning to embrace all the men in the world.

25

The following day, a Saturday morning, she opened the window and saw the wonderfully blue sky. She felt happy and gay, and out of nowhere she said to Jean-Marc, who was about to leave: "What do you suppose my poor Britannicus is up to these days?"

"Why?"

"Is he still horny? Is he still alive?"

"What makes you think of him?"

"I don't know. Just like that."

Jean-Marc left, and she was alone. She went into the bathroom, then over to her wardrobe, with the idea of making herself very beautiful. She looked at the shelves and something caught her attention. On the lingerie shelf, on top of a pile, her shawl lay neatly folded, whereas she recalled having tossed it in there carelessly. Did someone tidy up her things? The cleaning woman comes once a week and never touches her shelves. She marveled at her talent for observation and told herself she owed it to the training she got years back during her stays at the country house. She always felt so spied on down there that she learned to keep track of exactly how she had arranged her things, so as to spot the slightest change left by an alien hand. Delighted at the thought that those days were over, she checked herself with satisfaction in a mirror and left the apartment. Downstairs, she opened the mailbox, where a new letter awaited her. She put it into her bag and considered where she would go to read it. She found a small park and sat down beneath the enormous autumnal canopy of a yellowing lime tree set aglow by the sun.

". . . your heels tapping on the sidewalk make me think of the roads I never traveled, that stretch away like the boughs of a tree. You have reawakened the obsession of my early youth: I would imagine life before me like a tree. I used to call it the tree of possibilities. We see life that way for only a brief time. Thereafter, it comes to look like a track laid out once and for all, a tunnel one can never get out of. Still, the old specter of the tree stays with us in the form of an ineradicable nostalgia. You have made me remember that tree, and in return, I want to pass you its image, have you hear its enthralling murmur."

She raised her head. Above her, like a golden ceiling ornamented with birds, spread the lime tree's boughs. As if it were the same tree as the one the letter described. The metaphoric tree fused in her mind with her own old metaphor of the rose. She had to go home. In farewell she lifted her eyes again to the lime tree and went away.

Truth to tell, the mythologic rose of her adolescence did not procure her many adventures, and it does not even evoke any specific situation—apart from the rather droll recollection of an Englishman, much older than she, who at least ten years back had come into the agency on business and paid her court for half an hour. Only later did she learn of his renown as a womanizer, an orgiast. The encounter had no aftermath, except that it became a subject of jokes with Jean-Marc (he was the one who gave the fellow the nickname Britannicus) and that it lighted up for her a few words that until then had carried no special charge: the word "orgy," for instance, and the word "England," which, in contrast to what it evoked for others, to her represents the locus of pleasure and vice.

On the way home, she keeps hearing the ruckus of the birds from the lime tree and seeing the lecherous old Englishman; wrapped in the mists of these images, she moves at her leisurely pace until she comes to the street where she lives; some fifty meters ahead, the bistro tables have been set out on the sidewalk, and her young correspondent is sitting there, alone, without a book, without a newspaper, he's doing nothing, he has a glass of red wine in front of him and is staring into space with an expression of contented laziness that matches Chantal's. Her heart starts to pound. The whole thing is so devilishly neat! How could he have known that he would run into her just after she read his letter? On edge, as if she were walking naked under a red mantle, she draws closer to him, to the spy of her intimate life. She is only a few steps away and awaits the moment when he will address her. What will she do? She never wanted this encounter! But she cannot run off like a fearful little girl. Her steps grow slow, she tries not to look at him (good Lord, she really is behaving like a little girl, does that mean she has got so old?), but oddly, with divine unconcern, his glass of red in front of him, he sits gazing into space and seems not to see her.

She is already far past him, continuing her progress toward her house. Did du Barreau not dare? Or did he restrain himself? But no, no.

His unconcern was so genuine that Chantal can no longer doubt it: she was wrong; she was grotesquely wrong.

26

That evening she went to a restaurant with Jean-Marc. At the next table, a couple was plunged in a bottomless silence. Managing silence under the eyes of other people is not easy. Where should the two of them turn their gaze? It would be comical for them to look directly at each other and not say a word. Stare at the ceiling? That would seem to be making a display of their muteness. Observe the neighboring tables? They might intercept looks of amusement at their silence, and that would be still worse.

Jean-Marc said to Chantal: "Look, it's not that they hate each other. Or that apathy has replaced love. You can't measure the mutual affection of two human beings by the number of words they exchange. It's just that their heads are empty. It might even be out of tact that they're refusing to talk, if they've got nothing to say. The opposite of

78

my aunt in Périgord. Whenever I see her, she talks and talks without stop. I've tried to figure out the principle behind her volubility. She replicates in words absolutely everything she sees and everything she does. That she got up in the morning, that she had only black coffee for breakfast, that her husband went out for a walk afterward, imagine, Jean-Marc, when he got back he watched TV, imagine! he surfed it and then when he got tired of TV he flipped through some books. And—these are her words—that's how the time goes by for him. . . . You know, Chantal, I really like those simple, ordinary phrases that are a kind of definition of a mystery. That 'and that's how the time goes by for him' is a fundamental line. Their problem is time—how to make time go by, go by on its own, by itself, with no effort from them, without their being required to get through it themselves, like exhausted hikers, and that's why she talks, because the words she spouts manage inconspicuously to keep time moving along, whereas when her mouth stays closed, time comes to a standstill, emerges from the shadows huge and heavy, and it scares my poor aunt, who, in a panic, rushes to find someone she can tell how her daughter is having trouble with her child who's got diarrhea, yes, Jean-Marc, diarrhea, diarrhea, she went to the doctor, you don't know him, he lives not far from us, we know him for quite a while now, yes, Jean-Marc, quite a while, he's taken care of me too, this doctor, the winter I had that grippe, you remember, Jean-Marc, I had a horrible fever. . . ."

Chantal smiled, and Jean-Marc went on to another memory: "I had just turned fourteen, and my grandfather—not the cabinetmaker, the other one—was dying. There was a sound coming from his mouth that was unlike anything else, not even a moan because he wasn't in pain, not like words he might have been having trouble saying, no, he hadn't lost speech, just very simply he had nothing to say, nothing to communicate, no actual message, he didn't even have anyone to talk to, wasn't interested in anyone anymore, it was just him alone with the sound he was emitting, one sound, an 'ahhhh' that broke off only when he had to take a breath. I would watch him, hypnotized, and I never forgot that, because, though I was only a child, something seemed to become clear to me: this is existence as such confronting time as such; and that confrontation, I understood, is named boredom. My grandfather's bore-

80

dom expressed itself by that sound, by that endless 'ahhhh,' because without that 'ahhhh,' time
would have crushed him, and the only weapon
my grandfather had against time was that feeble
'ahhhh' going on and on."

"You mean he was dying and he was bored?"

"That's what I mean."

They talk on about death, about boredom, they
drink wine, they laugh, they have a good time,
they are happy.

Then Jean-Marc came back to his idea: "I'd
say that the quantity of boredom, if boredom is
measurable, is much greater today than it once
was. Because the old occupations, at least most
of them, were unthinkable without a passionate
involvement: the peasants in love with their land;
my grandfather, the magician of beautiful tables;
the shoemakers who knew every villager's feet by
heart; the woodsmen; the gardeners; probably
even the soldiers killed with passion back then.
The meaning of life wasn't an issue, it was there
with them, quite naturally, in their workshops, in
their fields. Each occupation had created its own
mentality, its own way of being. A doctor would
think differently from a peasant, a soldier would
behave differently from a teacher. Today we're

all alike, all of us bound together by our shared apathy toward our work. That very apathy has become a passion. The one great collective passion of our time."

Chantal said: "But still, tell me—you yourself, when you were a ski instructor, when you were writing for magazines on interior design or later on medicine, or maybe when you were working as a designer in a furniture studio . . ."

"Yes, I liked that best, but it didn't work out . . ."

"Or when you were out of work and doing nothing at all, you should have been bored, too!"

"Everything changed when I met you. Not because my little jobs became more exciting. But because everything that happens around me I turn into fodder for our conversations."

"We could talk about other things!"

"Two people in love, alone, isolated from the world, that's very beautiful. But what would they nourish their intimate talk with? However contemptible the world may be, they still need it to be able to talk together."

"They could be silent."

"Like those two, at the next table?" Jean-Marc laughed. "Oh, no, no love can survive muteness."

27

The waiter was leaning over their table with the dessert. Jean-Marc moved on to another topic: "You know that beggar we see now and then on our street?"

"No."

"Sure you do, you must have noticed him. That man in his forties who looks like a civil servant or a high-school teacher, and who's petrified with embarrassment when he holds out his hand to ask for a few francs. You don't know who I mean?"

"No."

"Yes! He always plants himself under a plane tree there, in fact the only one left on the street. You can see its foliage from our window."

The image of the plane tree, abruptly, brought the man to mind. "Ah yes! Now I know."

"I had this great urge to talk to him, to start a conversation, to find out more about him, but you have no idea how hard it is."

Chantal does not hear Jean-Marc's last words; she sees the beggar. The man beneath a tree. A diffident man whose reticence strikes the eye.

Always impeccably dressed, so that passersby barely understand that he is begging. A few months earlier, he spoke to her directly and, very politely, asked for aid.

Jean-Marc was still talking: "It's hard because he must be mistrustful. He wouldn't understand why I'd want to talk to him. Out of curiosity? That would scare him. Out of pity? That's humiliating. To make him some proposition? What should I propose? I tried to put myself in his shoes and understand what he might expect of people. I came up with nothing."

She pictures him under his tree, and it's the tree that suddenly, in a flash, brings home to her that this is the letter writer. His tree metaphor has given him away—him, the man under the tree, filled with the image of his tree. Her thoughts come rushing, one after the other: he's the only one, the man with no job and with all that free time, who could unobtrusively put a letter in her box, the only one who, shrouded in his nothingness, could follow her unnoticed in her daily rounds.

And Jean-Marc went on: "I could say to him, 'Come help me straighten up the basement.' He would refuse, not out of laziness but because he has no work clothes and needs to keep his suit in shape. Still, I'd really like to talk to him. Because he's my alter ego!"

Not listening to Jean-Marc, Chantal says: "What in the world could his sex life be like?"

"His sex life!" said Jean-Marc, laughing. "Zero, zero! Dreams!"

Dreams, thinks Chantal. So she's just the dream of some poor wretch. What made him choose her, her in particular?

And Jean-Marc, getting back to his idée fixe: "Someday I'd like to say to him, 'Come have a cup of coffee with me, you're my alter ego. You're living out the destiny I escaped by chance.'"

"Don't talk rubbish," Chantal says. "You weren't threatened with such a destiny."

"I never forget the moment when I quit medical school and realized that all the trains had left."

"Yes, I know, I know," says Chantal, who had heard this story many times, "but how can you compare your little setback with the real misfortunes of a man who stands and waits for a passerby to put a franc in his hand?"

"It's not a setback to give up your studies, what I gave up at that moment was ambition. I was suddenly a man without ambition. And having lost my ambition, I suddenly found myself at the margin of the world. And, what was worse: I had no desire to be anywhere else. I had all the less desire given that there was no real threat of hardship. But if you have no ambition, if you're not avid to succeed, to gain recognition, you're setting yourself up on the verge of ruin. True, I set myself up there in comfortable conditions. But still, it's the verge of ruin I'm set up on. So it's no exaggeration to say that I belong with that beggar and not with the owner of this magnificent restaurant where I'm having such a grand time."

Chantal thinks: I've become the erotic idol of a beggar. Now, there's a joke of an honor. Then she corrects herself: why should a beggar's desires be any less worthy of respect than those of a businessman? Since they're hopeless, the beggar's desires have one feature that's beyond price: they are free and sincere.

Then another idea occurs to her: the day she made love with Jean-Marc wearing the red nightgown, that third presence who was observing them, who was with them, wasn't the young man from the bistro, it was this beggar! Actually, he's the one who threw the red mantle over her shoulders, who turned her into a lecherous cardinal!

For the space of a few seconds, the idea feels painful to her, but her sense of humor quickly prevails, and in her inmost heart, silently, she laughs. She imagines this profoundly timid man, with his heartbreaking necktie, flattened against the wall of her bedroom, his hand out, fixedly and lecherously watching them romp in front of him. She imagines herself, once the love scene is over, climbing off the bed naked and sweaty, picking up her purse from the table, looking for some change, and putting it in his hand. She can barely contain her laughter.

28

Jean-Marc was watching Chantal, whose face suddenly brightened with a secret amusement. He did not want to ask her the reason, content to savor the pleasure of watching her. As she lost herself in her comic imaginings, he reflected that she was his sole emotional link to the world. People talk to him about prisoners, about the persecuted, about the hungry? He knows the only way he feels personally, painfully touched by their misfortune: he imagines Chantal in their place. People tell him about women raped in some civil war? He sees Chantal there, raped. She and she alone releases him from his apathy. Only through her can he feel compassion.

He would have liked to tell her this, but he was ashamed of the pathetic. The more so because another idea, completely opposite, caught him by surprise: what if he should lose this one person who binds him to humankind? He was thinking not of her death but of something subtler, something elusive that has been haunting him lately: that one day he wouldn't recognize her; that one day he would notice that Chantal was not the Chantal he lived with but that woman on the beach he mistook for her; that the certainty Chantal represented for him would turn out to be illusory, and that she would come to mean as little to him as everybody else.

She took his hand: "What's wrong with you? You're sad again. For the last couple of days I've noticed you're sad. What's wrong with you?"

"Nothing, nothing at all."

"Sure there is. Tell me, what's making you sad just now?"

"I imagined you were someone else."

"What?"

"That you're different from what I imagine you. That I'm wrong about your identity."

"I don't understand."

He saw a pile of brassieres. A sad little hill of brassieres. A silly hill. But right through that vision he immediately caught sight of the real face of Chantal as she sat across from him. He felt the touch of her hand on his, and the sense of having a stranger, or a traitor, before him vanished rapidly. He smiled: "Forget that. I didn't say a thing."

29

His back flat against the wall of the room where they were making love, his hand outstretched, his eyes fixed avidly on their naked bodies: during dinner at the restaurant, that is how she imagined him. Now his back is flat against the tree, his hand clumsily outstretched toward the passersby. At first she means to behave as though she hasn't noticed him; then, purposely, intentionally, with a vague notion of

89

slicing through a tangled situation, she stops in front of him. Without raising his eyes, he repeats his line: "I beg you to help me."

She looks at him: he is anxiously tidy, he is wearing a necktie, his salt-and-pepper hair is combed back. Is he handsome, is he ugly? His circumstances place him beyond the handsome and the ugly. She would like to say something to him, but she does not know what. Her discomfiture keeping her from speaking, she opens her purse, searches for change, but except for a few centimes she finds nothing. He stands there immobile, the terrible palm stretched toward her, and his immobility makes the silence weightier yet. To say at this point, "Excuse me, I have nothing on me," seems impossible, so she decides to give him a banknote, but she finds only a two-hundred-franc bill; it is an excessive offering and it makes her flush: to her mind she looks like a woman keeping an imaginary lover, overpaying him to write love letters to her. When instead of a little chip of cold metal the beggar feels paper in his hand, he raises his head, and she sees his utterly astonished eyes. It is a terrified look, and, uneasy, she moves quickly away.

When she put the banknote in his hand, she

still thought she was giving it to her admirer. Only as she hurries off does she become capable of a bit more clearheadedness: there was no gleam of complicity in his eyes; no mute allusion to an adventure shared; nothing but authentic and total surprise; the frightened astonishment of a poor man. Suddenly everything is obvious: to take that man for the author of the letters is the height of absurdity. She is overwhelmed with rage against herself. Why is she paying so much attention to this bullshit? Why, even in imagination, is she lending herself to this little adventure set up by a bored layabout with nothing to do? The idea of the bundle of letters hidden beneath her brassieres abruptly strikes her as unbearable. She pictures a person in some secret cranny observing her every move but unaware of her thoughts. Judging by what he saw, he could only think her a conventionally man-starved woman—worse, a romantic and stupid woman who worships every love letter as a sacred object and daydreams over it.

No longer able to stand the invisible observer's sneering gaze, as soon as she reaches home she goes to the wardrobe. She sees the pile of her brassieres and is struck by something. Yes, of course, she had already noticed it yesterday: her shawl was folded, not just tossed down as she had left it. In her euphoric state at the time she had immediately forgotten that. But now she cannot ignore this sign of a hand not her own. Ah, it's too obvious! He's read the letters! He's watching her! He's spying on her!

She is full of rage at a dozen different targets: at the unknown man unapologetically pestering her with letters; at herself for foolishly keeping them hidden; and at Jean-Marc for spying on her. She pulls out the bundle and goes (that makes how many times now!) into the bathroom. There, before ripping them up and sending them off with the water, she looks at them for the last time and, mistrustful now, finds the handwriting suspicious. She examines them carefully: the same ink throughout, and the characters are all very large, tilted slightly to the left, but different from one letter to the next, as if whoever wrote them could not keep to a consistent handwriting. The observation seems so strange to her that, once again, she does not tear up the letters, and she sits down at the table to reread them. She stops at the second one, which describes her on her trip to the dry cleaner's: how had that gone at the time? she was with Jean-Marc; he was the one carrying the valise. Inside the shop, she remembers very well, it was Jean-Marc who made the woman laugh. Her correspondent mentions the laughter. But how could he have heard it? He says he was looking at her from the street. But who could have watched her without her realizing it? Not du Barreau. Not the beggar. Only one person: the one who was with her inside the dry cleaner's. And the line "something added on to your life," which she had taken for a clumsy attack on Jean-Marc, was actually a narcissistic bit of coyness from Jean-Marc himself. Yes, he gave himself away by his narcissism, a plaintive narcissism meant to tell her: no sooner does some other man turn up in your path than I'm just a useless object added on to your life. Then she recalls that curious remark at the end of their dinner at the restaurant. He told her that he might have been mistaken about her identity. That she might be someone else! "I follow you around like a spy," he wrote her in the first letter. So he's the spy. He scrutinizes her, he does experiments on her to prove that she's not what he thought she was! He writes her letters under the name of some unknown person and then watches her behavior, he spies on her right down to her wardrobe, right down to her brassieres!

But why is he doing that?

There is only one possible answer: he is trying to trap her.

But why would he want to trap her?

To get rid of her. The fact is, he's younger than she, and she has gotten old. It's no good hiding her hot flashes, she's gotten old and it shows. He is looking for a reason to leave her. He couldn't say: You've gotten old and I'm young. He's too correct for that, too nice. But as soon as he's sure she is betraying him, that she is capable of betraying him, he will leave her with the same ease, the same coldness, as when he put his very old friend F. out of his life. That coldness, so oddly cheerful, has always frightened her. Now she sees that her fear was a forewarning.

30

He had inscribed Chantal's flush on the very opening page of the golden album of their love. They met for the first time in the midst of a great many people, in a reception room around a long table covered with glasses of champagne and platters of toast squares and terrines and ham. It was a mountain hotel, he was a ski instructor at the time, and he was invited, by chance and for that one evening, to join the participants of a conference that ended each evening with a little cocktail party. He was introduced to her in passing, so quickly they hadn't even the chance to catch each other's names. With other people around, they did not manage to exchange more than a few words. Jean-Marc returned uninvited the next day, solely to see her again. Spotting him, she flushed. She was red not only on her cheeks, but on her neck, and lower still, down to the low neckline of her dress, she turned magnificently red for all to see, red because of him and for him. That flush was her declaration of love, that flush decided everything. Thirty minutes later, they managed to meet alone in the dimness of a long corridor; without a word, avidly, they kissed.

The fact that thereafter, for years, he never saw her flush again was to him proof of the extraordinary nature of that flush back then, which glowed in their faraway past like a priceless ruby. Then, one day, she told him that men no longer turned to look at her. The words, in themselves insignificant, became important because of the flush that accompanied them. He could not be deaf to the language of colors, which was part of their love and which, linked to her phrase, seemed to him to speak of the distress of aging. That is why, disguised as a stranger, he wrote her: "I follow you around like a spy—you are beautiful, very beautiful."

When he put the first letter in the box, he was not even thinking of sending her others. He had no plan, he intended no future, he simply wanted to give her pleasure, right then, immediately, to rid her of the depressing sense that men no longer turned to look at her. He did not try to foresee her reactions. If, however, he had attempted to guess them, he would have supposed that she would show him the letter, saying, "Look! Men haven't forgotten about me yet after all!" and with the great innocence of a man in love, he would have added his own praises to those of the unknown writer. But she showed him nothing. Without a final dot, the episode stayed open. Over the next days, he caught her in despair, prey to thoughts of death, so that, want to or not, he went on.

As he wrote the second letter, he said to himself:

I'm becoming Cyrano; Cyrano: the man who declares himself to the woman he loves from behind the mask of another man; who, relieved of his own name, sees the explosion of his suddenly liberated eloquence. Thus, at the end of that letter, he added the signature "C.D.B." It was a code for him alone. As if he wanted to leave a secret mark of his existence. C.D.B.: Cyrano de Bergerac.

Cyrano he continued to be. Suspecting her of having lost faith in her charms, he described her body to her. He tried to note each part—face, nose, eyes, neck, legs—to make her proud of it again. He was happy to see that she dressed with greater pleasure, that she was more cheerful, but at the same time his success stung him: before, she had not liked to wear the red beads around her neck, even when he asked her to; and now it was another man she was obeying.

Cyrano cannot live without jealousy. The day he unexpectedly entered the bedroom where Chantal was leaning into a wardrobe shelf, he did notice her discomfiture. He talked about the eyelid washing the eye and pretended to have seen nothing; only the next day, when he was alone at home, did he open the wardrobe and find his two letters beneath the pile of brassieres.

Then, turning pensive, he wondered again why she had not shown them to him; the answer seemed simple. If a man writes letters to a woman, his point is to prepare the ground for approaching her later to seduce her. And if the woman keeps those letters secret, it is because she wants today's discretion to protect tomorrow's adventure. And if she saves them besides, it means she is prepared to see that future adventure as a love affair.

He stood for a long while before the open wardrobe, and after that, whenever he put a new letter into the box, he would go to check if he would find it in its place, beneath the brassieres.

31

If Chantal should learn that Jean-Marc was unfaithful to her, she would suffer, but it would square with what she could, just conceivably, expect from him. This espionage, though, this coplike testing he was putting her through, matched nothing she knew about him. When they met, he wanted to know nothing, hear nothing, about her past life. She quickly fell into line with the radicalism of that refusal. She never had any secrets from him and suppressed only what he himself did not wish to hear. She sees no reason why, all at once, he has begun to suspect her, to keep watch on her.

Then, suddenly, she remembers how those words about crimson cardinal garb aroused her, and she is ashamed: how receptive she's been to images someone sows in her head! how ridiculous she must have seemed to him! He has put her in a cage like a rabbit. Cruel and amused, he is observing her reactions.

And suppose she is wrong? Hasn't she been mistaken twice already when she thought she had unmasked her correspondent?

She goes to find some letters Jean-Marc wrote her in the past and compares them with those from C.D.B. Jean-Marc's handwriting leans slightly to the right, with fairly small characters, whereas in all the letters from the stranger the writing is sizable and leans to the left. But it is precisely that too-obvious dissimilarity that gives away the hoax. A person trying to disguise his handwriting will think first of changing the slant and the size. Chantal tries to compare the "f," the "a," the "o" as they appear in Jean-Marc's hand

99

and in the stranger's. She sees that despite their different sizes, their forms look fairly similar. But as she goes on comparing them, over and over, she grows less certain. Oh no, she's not a graphologist, and she cannot be sure of a thing.

She chooses a letter from Jean-Marc and one signed C.D.B.; she puts them into her handbag. What to do with the others? Find them a better hiding place? Why bother? Jean-Marc knows them, and he even knows where she puts them. She must not let him know that she feels herself under surveillance. She sets them back in the wardrobe exactly where they were all along.

Then she rang at the door of a graphology service. A young man in dark clothing greeted her and ushered her along a corridor into an office where, behind a table, was seated another man, brawny and in shirtsleeves. The young man stood leaning against the back wall of the room, while the brawny fellow rose and offered his hand.

He sat back down and she took an armchair across from him. She laid the letters from Jean-Marc and from C.D.B. on the table; when she explained, with some embarrassment, what she wanted to know, the man said, his tone quite remote: "I can give you a psychological analysis of the man whose identity you know. But it is difficult to do a psychological analysis of faked handwriting."

"I don't need a psychological analysis. I'm quite familiar with the psychology of the man who wrote these letters, if, as I think, he did write them."

"What you want, if I understand you, is certainty that the person who wrote that letter—your lover or your husband—is the same person who's changed his handwriting in this other one. You want to trip him up."

"That's not exactly it," she says, uncomfortable.

"Not exactly, but nearly. However, madame, I am a graphologist-psychologist, I am not a private eye, nor do I collaborate with the police."

Silence fell in the little room, and neither of the two men chose to break it, because neither one felt any compassion for her.

Within her body she sensed a wave of heat rise, a powerful, ferocious, expanding wave, she was red, red over her whole body; once again the words about the crimson cardinal's mantle crossed her mind, because in fact her body was now swathed in a sumptuous mantle stitched of flames.

"You've come to the wrong place," he went on. "This is not an informers' office."

She heard the word "informer," and her mantle of flames turned into a mantle of shame. She rose to take back her letters. But before she could manage to gather them up, the young man who had let her in stepped behind the table; standing near the brawny man, he looked carefully at the two handwritings, and "Of course it's the same person," he said; then, directly to her: "Look at this 't,' look at this 'g'!"

Suddenly she recognizes him: this young man is the waiter at the café in that Normandy town where she was waiting for Jean-Marc. And as she recognizes him, within her fiery body she hears her own astonished voice: But this whole thing, this isn't real! I'm hallucinating, I'm hallucinating, it can't be real!

The young man raised his head, looked at her (as if he meant to show her his face and be clearly recognized), and said, his smile at once gentle and disdainful: "Sure it is! It's the same handwriting. He's just made it bigger and slanted it to the left."

She does not want to hear any more, the word "informer" has banished every other word. She

102

feels like a woman denouncing the man she loves to the police, displaying as evidence a hair found in the adulterous bedsheets. Finally, after picking up her letters, without a word, she turns on her heel to leave. Once again the young man has changed position: he is at the door and opening it for her. She is six steps away, and that little distance seems infinite. She is red, she is burning, she is drenched in sweat. The man before her is arrogantly young and, arrogantly, he is staring at her poor body. Her poor body! Under the young man's gaze she feels it aging visibly, at a faster rate, and in plain daylight.

This seems to her the same situation she lived through in the café at the Normandy shore when, wearing that obsequious smile, he blocked her way to the door and she feared she would not be able to leave. She waits for him to pull the same trick, but, politely, he stands still beside the office door and lets her go through; then, with the faltering step of an old woman, she moves down the hallway to the street door (she feels his gaze pressing on her damp back), and when she is finally outside on the doorstep she has the sensation of having escaped a huge peril.

32

That day when they were walking together in the street, without speaking, seeing only unknown passersby around them, why did she suddenly flush? It was incomprehensible: taken aback, he could not control his reaction at the time: "You're flushing! How come?" She did not answer, and he was disturbed to see that something was happening in her which he knew nothing about.

As if that episode had rekindled the royal color from the golden album of their love, he wrote her the letter about the cardinal's crimson mantle. In his Cyrano role, he then pulled off his greatest feat: he captivated her. He was proud of his letter, of his seduction, but he felt a greater jealousy than ever. He was creating a phantom of a man and, without meaning to, was thus putting Chantal to a test that gauged her susceptibility to seduction by a man other than himself.

His jealousy was not the same sort as he had known in his youth when his imagination would set off an agonizing erotic fantasy; this was less painful but more destructive: very gradually, it was transforming a beloved woman into the simulacrum of a beloved woman. And since she was no longer a reliable person for him, there was now no stable point in the valueless chaos that is the world. Faced with this transsubstantiated (or desubstantiated) Chantal, he felt a strange melancholy apathy overtake him. Not apathy about her but apathy about everything. If Chantal is a simulacrum, then so is the whole of Jean-Marc's life.

In the end, his love prevailed over his jealousy and his doubts. He leaned into the open wardrobe, staring at the brassieres, and suddenly, without knowing how it came about, he was moved. Moved in the face of this immemorial action of women hiding a letter among their undergarments, this action by which the unique and inimitable Chantal takes her place in the endless procession of her peers. He had never wanted to know anything about the part of her intimate life that he had not shared with her. Why should he take an interest now, still less take offense at it?

Anyhow, he asked himself, what is an intimate secret? Is that where we hide what's most mysterious, most singular, most original about a human being? Are her intimate secrets what make Chantal the unique being he loves? No. What peo-

105

ple keep secret is the most common, the most ordinary, the most prevalent thing, the same thing everybody has: the body and its needs, its maladies, its manias—constipation, for instance, or menstruation. We ashamedly conceal these intimate matters not because they are so personal but because, on the contrary, they are so lamentably impersonal. How can he resent Chantal for belonging to her sex, for resembling other women, for wearing a brassiere and along with it the brassiere psychology? As if he didn't himself belong to some eternal masculine idiocy! They both of them got their start in that putterer's workshop where their eyes were botched with the disjointed action of the eyelid and where a reeking little factory was installed in their bellies. They both of them have bodies where their poor souls have almost no room. Shouldn't they forgive that in each other? Shouldn't they move beyond the little weaknesses they're hiding at the bottom of drawers? He was gripped by an enormous compassion, and to draw a final line under that whole story, he decided to write her one last letter.

33

Bent over a sheet of paper, he reflects again on what the Cyrano he was (and is again, for the last time) called "the tree of possibilities." The tree of possibilities: life as it reveals itself to a man arriving, astonished, at the threshold of his adult life: an abundant treetop canopy filled with bees singing. And he thinks he understands why she never showed him the letters: she wanted to hear the murmur of the tree by herself, without him, because he, Jean-Marc, represented the abolition of all possibilities, he was the reduction (even though it was a happy reduction) of her life to a single possibility. She could not tell him about the letters because that openness would have been an immediate indication (to herself and to him) that she was not really interested in the possibilities the letters promised her, that she was renouncing in advance that forgotten tree he was showing her. How could he resent that? After all, he is the one who wanted her to hear the music of a murmuring treetop. So she has behaved according to Jean-Marc's wishes. She has obeyed him.

Bent over his paper, he thinks: the echo of that

murmur must stay with Chantal even if the letter adventure comes to an end. And he writes her that an unexpected obligation requires him to go away. Then he adds a nuance to his statement: "Is this departure really unexpected or, rather, did I not write these letters precisely because I knew they would have no aftermath? Wasn't it the certainty of my departure that allowed me to speak to you with utter candor?"

Going away. Yes, that's the only possible denouement, but go where? He considers. What about not naming the destination? That would be a little too romantically mysterious. Or impolitely evasive. True, his existence must remain murky, he cannot give reasons for his departure because they would hint at the imaginary identity of the correspondent—his profession, for instance. Still, it would be more natural to say where he is going. A city within France? No. That would not be reason enough to break off a correspondence. He would have to go far away. New York? Mexico? Japan? That would be a little suspicious. Better to pick a city that is foreign and yet nearby, unremarkable. London! Of course; that seems so logical, so natural, that he says to himself with a smile: in fact, I can only go to London. And then wonders immediately: why exactly does London seem so natural to me? Thereupon arises the memory of the man from London about whom he and Chantal have often joked, the ladies' man who once gave Chantal his visiting card. The Englishman, the Britisher, whom Jean-Marc nicknamed Britannicus. It's not bad: London, the city of lascivious dreams. That's where the unknown worshiper will go to lose himself in the mob of orgiasts, chasers, pickup artists, erotomaniacs, perverts, lechers; that's where he will disappear forever.

And he thinks further: he'll leave the word "London" in his letter as a kind of signature, like a barely perceptible trace of his conversations with Chantal. Silently, he makes fun of himself: he wants to remain unknown, unidentifiable, because the game requires that. And yet a contrary desire— a desire totally unjustified, unjustifiable, irrational, murky, certainly stupid—incites him to not go completely unseen, to leave a mark, to hide somewhere a coded signature by which an unknown and exceptionally clear-sighted observer could identify him.

Descending the staircase to put the letter in the box, he heard shrill voices shouting. Downstairs, he saw them: a woman with three children at the doorbell buttons. Heading for the boxes along the facing wall, he passed beside them. When he turned around, he saw that the woman was pressing on the button bearing his name and Chantal's.

"Are you looking for someone?" he asked.

The woman told him a name.

"That's me!"

She took a step back and looked at him with obvious admiration: "It's you! Oh, I'm happy to meet you! I'm Chantal's sister-in-law!"

34

Disconcerted, he could do no other than invite them upstairs.

"I don't want to bother you," said the sister-in-law when they all entered the apartment.

"You're not bothering me. And anyhow, Chantal won't be long."

The sister-in-law began to talk; from time to time she would throw a glance at the children, who were very quiet, shy, almost dumbstruck.

"I'm glad Chantal will see them," she said, caressing the head of one of them. "She doesn't even know them, they were born after she left. She liked children. Our country house overflowed with them. Her husband was pretty ghastly. I shouldn't talk this way about my own brother, but he remarried and he never sees us anymore." Laughing: "Actually, I always liked Chantal better than her husband!"

Again she stepped back and stared at Jean-Marc, her look both admiring and flirtatious: "Well, she certainly knew how to pick the next man! I've come to tell you you're welcome at our place. I'd be grateful if you came, and brought our Chantal back to us at the same time. The house is open to you whenever you like. Always."

"Thank you."

"You're a big man, how I love that. My brother is smaller than Chantal. I always had the feeling she was his mommy. She'd call him 'my little mousie'—just think, she gave him a girl's nickname! I always used to imagine," she said, bursting into laughter, "that she'd hold him in her arms and rock him and whisper 'my little mousie, my little mousie!'"

She did a few dancing steps, her arms crooked as if she were carrying a baby, and repeated, "My little mousie, little mousie!" She continued her dance another brief moment, to urge an answering laugh from Jean-Marc. To satisfy her, he faked a smile and imagined Chantal with a man she called "my mousie." The sister-in-law went on talking, and he could not rid himself of that exasperating image: the image of Chantal calling a man (smaller than she) "my little mousie."

Noise came from the next room. Jean-Marc realized that the children were no longer here with them; that was the cunning strategy of the invaders: under cover of their insignificance, they managed to slip into Chantal's room; at first silent like a secret army and then, having discreetly shut the door behind them, with the *furioso* of conquerors.

It worried Jean-Marc, but the sister-in-law reassured him: "It's nothing. They're children. They're playing."

"Well, sure," said Jean-Marc. "I see that they're playing," and he headed for the bedroom din. The sister-in-law was faster. She opened the door: they had turned the swivel chair into a merry-go-round; one child lay flat on his stomach on the seat, he was spinning around, and the two others were watching him and shouting.

"See, they're playing, I told you," the sister-in-law repeated as she closed the door. Then, with a wink of collusion: "They're children. What do you expect? It's too bad Chantal's not here. I'd so like her to see them."

The noise from the next room was becoming pandemonium, and Jean-Marc suddenly lost any desire to quiet the children down. He sees before him a Chantal who, amid the family mob, cradles a little man she called "mousie." The image comes together with another one: Chantal jealously protecting an unknown worshiper's letters so as not to nip in the bud a promise of adventure. That Chantal is unfamiliar; that Chantal is not the woman he loves; that Chantal is a simulacrum. A strange destructive desire fills him, and he relishes the racket the children are making. He wants them to demolish the room, demolish the whole little world that he used to love and that has become a simulacrum.

"My brother," the sister-in-law was saying meanwhile, "was too puny for her, you know what I mean, puny . . ." she said, laughing, ". . . in every sense of the word. You know, you know!" She laughed again. "In fact, can I give you a piece of advice?"

"If you want."

"Very intimate advice!"

She brought her mouth close and said something, but her lips made a noise as they touched Jean-Marc's ear and made her words inaudible.

She pulled back and laughed: "What do you say to that?"

He had caught none of it, but he laughed too.

"Ah, that really tickled you!" said the sister-in-law, adding: "I could tell you lots of things like that. Oh, you know, she and I had no secrets from each other. If you run into any problems with her, tell me: I can give you some good tips!" She laughed: "I know what it takes to tame her!"

And Jean-Marc thinks: Chantal has always spoken with hostility of her sister-in-law's family. How can the sister-in-law show such clear affection for her? What exactly does it mean, then, that Chantal hated them? How can a person hate a thing and at the same time adapt to it so readily?

In the next room the children were rampaging, and the sister-in-law, gesturing in their direction, smiled: "That doesn't disturb you, I see! You're like me. You know, I'm not a real orderly woman, I like things to move, I like things to change, I like things to sing—I mean, I like life!"

Against the background of shouting children,

his thoughts continue: that facility she has for adapting to things she detests, is that really so admirable? Is having two faces such a triumph? He used to relish the idea that among the advertising people she was like an interloper, a spy, a masked enemy, a potential terrorist. But she isn't a terrorist, she's more of a—if he has to resort to such political terminology—a collaborationist. A collaborationist who serves a detestable power without identifying with it, who works for it while keeping separate from it, and who one day, standing before her judges, will defend herself by claiming that she had two different faces.

35

Chantal stopped in the doorway and stood there, astonished, for almost a minute, because neither Jean-Marc nor her sister-in-law was noticing her. She heard the clarion voice that she had not heard for so long: ". . . You're like me. You know, I'm not a real orderly woman, I like things to move, I like things to change, I like things to sing—I mean, I like life!"

115

At last her sister-in-law's eyes landed on her: "Chantal!" she cried. "Isn't this a surprise?" and she rushed to embrace her. At the crease of her lips Chantal felt the wetness of her sister-in-law's mouth.

The awkwardness brought on by Chantal's arrival was soon interrupted by the irruption of a kid into the room. "Here's our little Corinne," the sister-in-law announced to Chantal; then, to the child: "Say hello to your aunt," but the child paid no attention to Chantal and announced that she had to make peepee. The sister-in-law, without hesitating, as if she were already quite familiar with the apartment, went off with Corinne down the corridor and vanished into the bathroom.

"God," murmured Chantal, taking advantage of the sister-in-law's absence, "how did they track us down?"

Jean-Marc shrugged his shoulders. The sister-in-law had left the corridor and the bathroom doors wide open, so they couldn't say much to each other. They heard the urine splashing into the toilet bowl, mingling with the sister-in-law's voice giving them news of her family and every now and then urging the pisser along.

Chantal remembers: once, on a vacation at the

country house, she was inside the locked bathroom; suddenly someone tugged at the doorknob. Hating conversations through bathroom doors, she did not answer. From the other end of the house somebody shouted to quiet the impatient person at the door: "Chantal's in there!" Despite the information, the impatient person wrenched the doorknob several more times, as if to protest Chantal's muteness.

The noise of the urine is followed by the flush, and Chantal is still remembering the big concrete house where all the sounds carried and no one could tell what direction they came from. She was accustomed to hearing the coital sighs of her sister-in-law (their unnecessary loudness was certainly intended to function as a provocation, less sexual than moral: as a demonstration of the rejection of all secrets); one day, the love sighs reached her again and only after some time did she realize that an asthmatic grandmother was wheezing and moaning at the other end of that echoing house.

The sister-in-law came back into the living room. "Go on," she said to Corinne, who ran off into the next room to rejoin the other children. Then she spoke to Jean-Marc: "I don't reproach Chantal for leaving my brother. Maybe she should have done it sooner. But I do reproach her for forgetting about us." And, turning to Chantal: "After all, Chantal, we do represent a big piece of your life! You can't repudiate us, erase us, you can't change your past! Your past is what it is. You can't deny you were happy with us. I've come to tell your new companion that you're both welcome at my place!"

Chantal was hearing her talk and thinking that she had lived too long with that family without displaying her otherness, so her sister-in-law was (almost) justifiably upset that after Chantal's divorce she had broken off all ties with them. Why had she been so nice, so acquiescent during her married years? She didn't know, herself, what to call her attitude of the time. Docility? Hypocrisy? Apathy? Self-control?

When her son was alive, she was fully prepared to accept that life in a collective, under constant scrutiny, with the collective sloppiness, the nearly obligatory nudism around the pool, the guileless lack of privacy that told her, by subtle yet astonishing traces, who had been in the bathroom before her. Did she enjoy that? No, she was filled with disgust, but it was a mild, quiet, noncombative, resigned, almost peaceful disgust, a little sardonic, never rebellious. If her child had not died, she would have lived that way to the end of her days.

In Chantal's room, the racket intensified. The sister-in-law shouted: "Quiet!" but her voice was more jolly than angry and did not sound eager to calm the uproar so much as to join the fun.

Chantal loses patience and goes into her room. The children are clambering over the armchairs, but Chantal does not see them; transfixed, she is staring at the wardrobe; its door is gaping open; and in front of it, on the floor, her brassieres and underpants are scattered, along with the letters. Only then does she notice that the eldest of the children has twisted a brassiere around her head so that the pocket meant for the breast is standing up atop her hair like a cossack's helmet.

"Just look at that!" the sister-in-law says, laughing and holding Jean-Marc chummily by the shoulder. "Look, look! It's a masquerade party!"

Chantal sees the letters tossed to the floor. Fury rises to her head. It's barely an hour since she left the graphologist's office, where she was treated with contempt and, betrayed by her flaming body, had been unable to stand up for herself.

Now she's sick of feeling guilty: these letters no longer represent a foolish secret she should be ashamed of; henceforward they symbolize Jean-Marc's deceitfulness, his perfidy, his treason.

The sister-in-law caught Chantal's glacial reaction. Still talking and laughing, she leaned toward the child, unbound the brassiere, and stooped to collect the underwear.

"No, no, please, leave them," Chantal told her, in a firm tone.

"As you like, as you like, I was willing to do it."

"I know," said Chantal, looking at her sister-in-law, who went back to lean on Jean-Marc's shoulder; it occurs to Chantal that they go well together, that they make a perfect couple, a couple of overseers, a couple of spies. No, she has no wish to shut the wardrobe door. She is leaving it open as proof of the pillage. She says to herself: this apartment belongs to me, and I have an enormous desire to be alone in it; to be superbly, supremely alone. And aloud she says: "This apartment belongs to me, and no one has the right to open my wardrobes and rummage in my personal things. No one. I repeat: No one."

That last word was aimed far more at Jean-Marc than at her sister-in-law. But lest she give anything away in front of the intruder, she also spoke separately to her: "I'm asking you to leave."

"Nobody was rummaging in your personal things," said the sister-in-law defensively.

As her sole response, Chantal tipped her head toward the open wardrobe, with the underwear and the letters strewn on the floor.

"Good Lord, the children were playing!" said the sister-in-law, and as if they felt anger shivering in the air, the children followed their superb diplomatic instinct and kept still.

"I'm asking you," Chantal repeated, and she pointed to the door.

One of the children was holding an apple he had taken from a bowl on the table.

"Put the apple back where it was," Chantal told him.

"I'm dreaming!" cried the sister-in-law.

"Put the apple back. Who gave it to you?"

"She refuses a child an apple, I must be dreaming!"

The child put the apple back in the bowl, the sister-in-law took him by the hand, the other two joined them, and they went away.

36

She is alone with Jean-Marc and sees no difference between him and those who have just left.

"I had almost forgotten," she says, "that I
bought this apartment originally so as to be free
at last, to be not spied on, to be able to put my
things where I want and be sure that they will
stay right where I put them."

"I've told you many times that I belong with that
beggar and not with you. I'm at the margin of this
world. You, you've put yourself at the center of it."

"That's quite a plush marginality you've set
yourself up in, and it costs you nothing."

"I'm ready anytime to leave my plush marginality. But you, you'll never give up that citadel of
conformism where you've established yourself
with all your many faces."

37

A minute earlier, Jean-Marc had been hoping
to explain things, to acknowledge his hoax, but

that exchange of four retorts has made all dialogue impossible. He has nothing further to say, because it is true that this apartment does belong to her and not to him; she told him he had set himself up in quite a plush marginality that cost him nothing, and that's true: he earns a fifth of what she earns, and their whole relationship rests on the tacit agreement that they will never mention that inequality.

They were both standing, face-to-face with a table between them; she pulled an envelope from her bag, tore it open, and unfolded the letter inside; it was the one he had just written, scarcely an hour earlier. She hid nothing at all, and he understood that she was making a point. Without a qualm, she read before his eyes the letter that she should have kept secret. Then she put it back in her bag, gave Jean-Marc a brief, nearly indifferent glance, and without a word went into her room.

He considers again what she had said: "No one has the right to open my wardrobe and rummage in my personal things." So she has realized, God knows how, that he knows those letters and their hiding place. She means to show him that she knows he does and that the fact doesn't matter to her. That she is determined to live as she sees fit and without worrying about him. That from now on she is prepared to read her love letters in front of him. Her unconcern anticipates Jean-Marc's absence. For her he is no longer there. She has already evicted him.

She stayed in her room a long time. He could hear the furious voice of the vacuum cleaner bringing order back to the shambles the intruders had left there. Then she went into the kitchen. Ten minutes later, she called him. They sat down at the table to eat a small cold meal. For the first time in their life together, they said not a word. Oh, how rapidly they masticated food whose taste they never perceived! Again she withdrew into her room. Not knowing what to do (unable to do anything), he put on his pajamas and lay down in the wide bed where they usually lay together. But that evening she did not come out of her room. Time passed, and he was unable to sleep. Finally he got up and pressed his ear to her door. He heard regular breathing. That calm sleep, her ease at dropping off, tortured him. He stayed there a long time, his ear to the door, and he told himself that she was much less vulnerable than he had thought. And that perhaps he was wrong

when he had supposed her the weaker of them
and himself the stronger.

Actually, who is the stronger one? When they
were both out on the terrain of love, perhaps it
was really he. But with the terrain of love gone
from under their feet, she is the strong one, and
he is the weak.

38

There on her narrow bed, she did not sleep as
well as he thought; her sleep was a hundred times
interrupted and full of dreams that were unpleasant and disjointed, absurd, meaningless, and dis-
tressingly erotic. Each time she wakes after such
dreams, she feels uneasy. That, she thinks, is one
of the secrets of a woman's life, every woman's:
the nocturnal promiscuity that renders suspect
all promises of fidelity, all purity, all innocence.
In our century, nobody finds this offensive, but
Chantal likes to imagine the Princesse de Clèves,
or Bernardin de Saint-Pierre's chaste Virginie, or
Saint Theresa of Ávila, or, in our own day, Mother
Teresa running in a sweat through the world,

doing her good works—she likes to imagine them emerging from their nights as from a cloaca of unacknowledgeable, improbable, imbecilic vices, and by day turning back into virginal, virtuous women. Such was her night: she woke up several times, always after bizarre orgies with men she didn't know and found revolting.

Very early in the morning, not wishing to fall back into those dirty pleasures, she dressed and filled a little valise with a few items necessary for a short trip. Just as she was ready, she saw Jean-Marc in pajamas at the door of her room.

"Where are you going?" he asked.

"To London."

"What? To London? Why London?"

She said, very calmly: "You know very well why London." Jean-Marc flushed.

She repeated: "You know very well, don't you?" and she looked at his face. What a triumph for her to see that this time he was the one to turn all red!

His cheeks afire, he said: "No, I don't know why London."

She was delighted to see him flush. "We have a conference in London," she said. "I just learned about it last evening. You can understand that I

126

had neither the opportunity nor the desire to tell you about it."

She was sure that he could not possibly believe her and delighted that her lie should be so undisguised, so bold, so insolent, so hostile.

"I've called a taxi. I'm going down now. It should be here any minute."

She smiled at him the way one smiles farewell or goodbye. And at the last moment, as if it were against her intention, as if it were a gesture not in her control, she laid her right hand on Jean-Marc's cheek; this gesture was brief, it lasted only a second or two, then she turned her back on him and left.

39

He feels the touch of her hand on his cheek, or more precisely the touch of three fingertips, and the trace of it is cold, like after the touch of a frog. Her caresses were always slow, calm, it used to seem to him that they were meant to prolong time. Whereas these three fingers laid briefly on his cheek were not a caress but a reminder. As if a woman snatched up by a storm, carried off by a wave, could muster just one fleeting gesture to say: "And yet I was here! I did pass through! Whatever happens, don't forget me!"

Mechanically, he dresses and considers what they said about London. "Why London?" he asked, and she answered: "You know very well why London." That was a clear allusion to the departure he had announced in his last letter. That "you know very well" meant: you know that letter. But that letter, which she had just taken out of the box downstairs, could be known only to its sender and to her. In other words, Chantal had torn the mask off poor Cyrano and she was telling him: you yourself invited me to London, so I'm following your orders.

But if she has guessed (my God, my God, how could she have guessed?) that he is the one who wrote the letters, why is she taking it so badly? Why is she so cruel? If she has guessed it all, why hasn't she also guessed the reasons for his trickery? What does she suspect him of? Behind all these questions, there is one thing he's sure of: he does not understand her. For that matter, she hasn't understood anything either. Their ideas have gone in different directions, and it seems to him they will never converge again.

The pain he feels does not wish to heal; on the contrary, it seeks to aggravate the wound and parade it about the way one parades an injustice for all to see. He hasn't the patience to wait for Chantal's return to explain the source of the misunderstanding. Deep down he knows very well that this would be the only reasonable behavior, but pain doesn't listen to reason, it has its own reason, which is not reasonable. What his unreasonable reason wants is for Chantal, when she returns, to find the apartment empty, without him, as she proclaimed she wanted it in order to be alone there and away from espionage. He puts some banknotes in his pocket, all the money he has, then hesitates a moment over whether he should or should not take the keys. In the end he leaves them on the little table in the foyer. When she sees them, she will understand that he will not be back. Only a few jackets and shirts in the closet, only a few books in the bookcase, will still be here as mementos.

He goes out without knowing what he will do. The important thing is to leave that apartment which is no longer his. Leave it before deciding where he will go next. Not until he is in the street will he allow himself to give it some thought.

But once downstairs, he has the strange sensation of being outside reality. He has to stop in the middle of the sidewalk to be able to consider. Where to go? He has disparate ideas in his head: Périgord, where part of his peasant family lives and always welcomes him with pleasure; some cheap hotel in Paris. While he considers, a taxi stops at a red light. He waves it over.

40

Downstairs in the street, of course, no taxi was waiting for her, and Chantal had no idea where to go. Her decision was a total improvisation, spurred by the distress she was unable to master. At the moment, she wants only one thing: not to see him for at least a day and a night. She thought about taking a hotel room right here in Paris, but immediately the idea seemed foolish: what would she do all day? Walk in the streets and breathe their stench? Lock herself up in her room? And do what there? Then she thinks of taking the car and going off to the country, at random, finding a peaceful spot and staying there a day or two. But where?

Without knowing exactly how, she wound up near a bus stop. She felt like climbing aboard the first bus to pass and letting herself be carried to its terminus. One drew up and she was amazed to see that the list of stops included the Gare du Nord. The London trains leave from that station.

She has the impression of being drawn along by a conspiracy of coincidences and tries to see it as a good fairy coming to her aid. London: she had told Jean-Marc that that was where she was going, but only as a way of letting him know that she had unmasked him. Now an idea occurs to her: perhaps Jean-Marc took the London destination seriously; perhaps he's going to intercept her at the railroad station. And another idea follows that one, a weaker one, barely audible, like the voice of a tiny bird: if Jean-Marc is there, this odd misunderstanding will come to an end. The idea is like a caress, but too short a caress, because immediately thereafter she rebels against him again and rejects any nostalgia.

But where will she go and what will she do? Suppose she really did go to London? Suppose she let her lie become truth? She remembers that in her notebook she still has Britannicus' address. Britannicus: how old would he be now? She

knows that meeting him would be the least prob-
able thing in the world. So what? All the better.
She'll get to London, walk around there, take a
hotel room, and come back to Paris tomorrow.

Then that idea displeases her: in leaving the
apartment house, she thought she was taking
back her independence, whereas, in reality, she is
letting herself be manipulated by an unknown
and uncontrolled force. Leaving for London, a
decision suggested by preposterous chance, is
craziness. Why should she think that such a conspiracy of coincidences would be working in her
favor? Why take it for a good fairy? What if the
fairy is wicked and is conspiring toward her
ruin? She promises herself: when the bus stops
at the Gare du Nord, she won't move; she'll keep
riding.

But when the bus does stop there, she is surprised to find herself getting off. And as if sucked
along, she moves toward the railroad station.

In the enormous lobby, she sees the marble
staircase leading upward, toward the waiting
room for London passengers. She means to look
at the posted timetable, but before she manages
to do that, she hears her name, amid laughter.
She stops and sees her colleagues gathered at the

bottom of the staircase. When they realize that she has spotted them, their laughter becomes still louder. They are like teenagers who have pulled off a good prank, a wonderful bit of theater.

"We know what it takes to get you to come with us! If you'd known we were here, you would have made up some excuse, as always! Damned individualist!" And again they shout with laughter.

Chantal knew that Leroy was planning a conference in London, but it was not supposed to happen for another three weeks. How come they're here today? Once again she has the strange feeling that what is happening is not real, cannot be real. But that astonishment is instantly succeeded by another: contrary to everything she might herself have supposed, she feels sincerely happy about the presence of her colleagues, grateful to them for having set up this surprise.

As they climb the stairs, a young colleague takes her by the arm, and she thinks that Jean-Marc always drew her away from the life that ought to have been hers. She heard him saying: "You've put yourself at the center." And: "You've established yourself in a citadel of conformism." Now she retorts: Yes. And you won't stop me from staying there!

In the crowd of travelers, her young colleague, still arm in arm, draws her toward the police checkpoint at the staircase that leads down to the platform. As if intoxicated, she continues the silent quarrel with Jean-Marc and declares: What judge decreed that conformism is an evil and nonconformism is a good? Isn't conforming a way of drawing close to other people? Isn't conformism the great meeting place where everyone converges, where life is most dense, most ardent?

From the top of the staircase she sees the London train, modern and elegant, and she tells herself again: Whether it's good luck or bad to be born onto this earth, the best way to spend a life here is to let yourself be carried along, as I am at this moment, by a cheerful, noisy crowd moving forward.

41

Seated in the taxi, he said: "Gare du Nord!" and that was the moment of truth: he can quit the apartment, he can toss the keys into the Seine, sleep on the street, but he hasn't the strength to withdraw from her. Going to look for her at the station is an act of despair, but the train for London is the only indication, the only one she has given him, and Jean-Marc is not up to neglecting it, no matter how infinitesimal the probability that it will show him the right path.

When he reached the station, the London train was there. He climbed the stairs two at a time and bought his ticket; most of the passengers had already boarded; on the platform, which was under strict surveillance, he was the last to arrive; the whole length of the train, policemen patrolled with German shepherds trained to detect explosives; his car was full of Japanese with cameras slung from their necks; he found his seat and sat down.

Then he was struck by the absurdity of what he was doing. He's in a train where, in all likelihood, the woman he's seeking is not. In three hours, he will be in London with no idea why he's there; he has just enough to pay for the return trip. Distraught, he got up and stepped out onto the platform vaguely tempted to go back home. But how could he go back without the keys? He had left them on the little foyer table. Clearheaded again, he now knows that that gesture was only sentimental histrionics for his own eyes: the concierge had a duplicate and would readily give it to him. Wavering, he looked down to the end of the platform and saw that all the exits were closed. He stopped a guard and asked him how he might leave there; the guard said that it was no longer possible; for security reasons, once a person is on this train he cannot get off it; every passenger must stay there as living guarantee that he has not planted a bomb; there are Islamic terrorists and there are Irish terrorists; all they dream of is a massacre in the undersea tunnel.

He got back on the train, a woman taking tickets smiled at him, all the attendants smiled, and he thought: this, with more and bigger smiles, is how the rocket is launched into the tunnel of death, this rocket in which the warriors against boredom, American, German, Spanish, Korean tourists, are willing to risk their lives in their great battle. He sat down and, as soon as the train started, he got up and went to look for Chantal.

He entered a first-class car. On one side of the aisle there were lounge chairs for one person, on the other, for two; at the center of the car the chairs were turned face-to-face, and passengers in them were talking noisily together. Chantal was among them. He saw her from the back: he recognized the infinitely touching, almost funny, shape of her head with its outmoded chignon. Seated by the window, she was taking part in the conversation, which was lively; it could only be her colleagues from the agency; so then she hadn't lied? however improbable that might seem, no, certainly, she had not lied.

He stood unmoving; he heard much laughter and made out Chantal's. She was cheerful. Yes, she was cheerful, and that wounded him. He watched her gestures, and they were imbued with a liveliness he did not recognize in her. He could not hear what she was saying, but he saw her hand energetically rising and falling; he found it impossible to recognize that hand; it was the hand of someone else; he didn't feel that Chantal was betraying him, it was a different thing: he felt as if she no longer existed for him, had gone off somewhere, into some other life where, if he should meet her, he would no longer recognize her.

42

In a pugnacious tone of voice, Chantal said: "But how could a Trotskyite turn religious? Where's the logic?"

"My dear friend, you know Marx's famous line: change the world."

"Of course."

Chantal was seated by the window, across from the oldest of her agency colleagues, the refined lady with her ring-laden fingers; at her side, Leroy went on talking: "Well, our century has made one enormous thing clear: man is not capable of changing the world and will never change it. That is the fundamental conclusion of my experience as a revolutionary. A conclusion that is, incidentally, tacitly accepted by everybody. But there is another one, which goes further. This one is theological, and it says: man has no right to change what God has created. We have to follow that injunction all the way."

Chantal watched him with delight: he was talking not as a giver of lessons but as a provocateur. This is what Chantal loves in him: that dry tone of a man for whom everything he does is a provocation in the hallowed tradition of revolutionaries or of the avant-garde; he never forgets to *"épater le bourgeois,"* even if he's reciting the most conventional verities. Besides, don't the most provocative verities ("The bourgeois to the gallows!") become the most official verities once they come to power? Convention can turn into provocation, and provocation into convention, at the drop of a hat. What matters is the determination to go to extremes with every position. Chantal imagines Leroy at the turbulent meetings of the 1968 student revolt, spouting in his intelligent, logical, dry style the maxims any commonsensical resistance was doomed to be defeated by: the bourgeoisie has no right to exist; art that the working class doesn't understand must disappear; science that serves the interests of the bourgeoisie is worthless; those who teach it must be thrown out of the university; no freedom for the enemies of freedom. The more absurd the proposition he was advancing, the prouder he was of it, because it takes a very great intelligence to breathe logical meaning into meaningless ideas.

Chantal answered: "All right, I agree that all change is noxious. Therefore, it would be our duty to protect the world against change. Alas, the world is incapable of stopping the insane rush of its transformations . . ."

". . . of which man is, however, a mere instrument," Leroy interrupted: "The invention of the locomotive contains the seed of the airplane's design, which leads ineluctably to the space rocket. That logic is contained in the things themselves, in other words, it is part of the divine project. You can turn in the whole human race for a different one, and still the evolution that leads from the bicycle to the rocket will be just the same. Man is only an operator, not the author of that evolution. And a paltry operator at that, since he doesn't know the meaning of what he's operating. That meaning doesn't belong to us, it belongs to God alone, and we're here only to obey Him so that He can do what He wants."

She shut her eyes: the sweet word "promiscuity" came to her mind and suffused her; she enunciated silently to herself: "promiscuity of ideas." How could such contradictory attitudes follow after one another in a single head like two mistresses in the same bed? In the past that nearly infuriated her, but today it entrances her: for she knows that the contrast between what Leroy used to say and what he's professing today doesn't matter in the slightest. Because one idea is as good as another. Because all statements and positions carry the same value, can rub against one another, nestle, snuggle, fondle, mingle, diddle, cuddle, couple.

A soft, slightly quavering voice rises up across from Chantal: "But in that case, why are we here below? Why are we living?"

It was the voice of the refined lady sitting beside Leroy, whom she adores. Chantal thinks how Leroy is at this moment flanked by two women he must choose between: a romantic one and a cynical one; she hears the lady's pleading little voice, reluctant to forgo her lovely beliefs but at the same time (in Chantal's fantasy) defending them with the unacknowledged hope of seeing them laid low by her demonic hero, who now turns to her:

"Why are we living? To provide God with human flesh. Because the Bible, my dear lady, does not ask us to seek the meaning of life. It asks us to procreate. Love one another and procreate. Understand this: the meaning of that 'love one another' is determined by that 'procreate.' That 'love one another' carries absolutely no implication of charitable love, of compassionate, spiritual, or passionate love, it only means very simply 'make love!' 'copulate!' (he drops his voice and leans toward her) 'fuck!'" (Like a devout disciple, docilely, the lady gazes into his eyes.) "That, and that alone, constitutes the meaning of human life. All the rest is bullshit."

Leroy's reasoning is dry as a razor, and Chantal agrees: love as an exaltation of two individuals, love as fidelity, passionate attachment to a single person—no, that doesn't exist. And if it does exist, it is only as self-punishment, willful blindness, escape into a monastery. She tells herself that even if it does exist, love ought not to exist, and the idea does not make her bitter, on the contrary, it produces a bliss that spreads throughout her body. She thinks of the metaphor of the rose that moves through all men and tells herself that she has been living locked away by love and now she is ready to obey the myth of the rose and merge with its giddy fragrance. At that point in her reflections, she remembers Jean-Marc. Is he still at home? Has he left? She wonders this with no emotion at all: as if she were wondering if it's raining in Rome or nice weather in New York.

Still, however little he means to her, the memory of Jean-Marc had made her look around. At the end of the car, she saw someone turn his back and go into the next car. She thought she recognized Jean-Marc, trying to evade her glance. Had it actually been he? Rather than seek the answer, she looked out of the window: the landscape was getting uglier and uglier, the fields grayer and grayer, and the plains spiked by a greater and greater number of metal pylons, concrete structures, cables. A loudspeaker announced that in the next few seconds the train would go down beneath the sea. And in fact she saw a round black hole into which, like a snake, the train was about to glide.

43

"We're going down," said the refined lady, and her voice betrayed a fearful excitement.

"Into hell," added Chantal, who presumed that Leroy would have liked the lady to be even more naïve, even more astonished, even more fearful. She now felt herself to be his diabolical assistant. She enjoyed the idea of bringing this refined and prim lady to him in his bed, which she imagined not in some sumptuous London hotel but on a rostrum in the midst of fires and wailing and smoke and devils.

There was nothing to see through the window now, the train was in the tunnel, and she felt herself drawing far away from her sister-in-law, from Jean-Marc, from scrutiny, from espionage, drawing away from her life, from her life that stuck so to her, that weighed on her; the words "lost to sight" suddenly came to mind, and she was surprised to find that the journey toward disappearance was not gloomy, that under the aegis of her mythological rose, it was gentle and joyful.

"We're going deeper and deeper," said the lady, anxiously.

"To where truth resides," said Chantal.

"To where," added Leroy, "resides the answer to your question: why are we living? what is essential in life?" He looked hard at the lady. "The essential, in life, is to perpetuate life: it is childbirth, and what precedes it, coitus, and what precedes coitus, seduction, that is to say kisses, hair floating in the wind, silk underwear, well-cut brassieres, and everything else that makes people ready for coitus, for instance good chow—not

144

fine cuisine, a superfluous thing no one appreciates anymore, but the chow everyone buys—and along with chow, defecation, because you know, my dear lady, my beautiful adored lady, you know what an important position the praise of toilet paper and diapers occupies in our profession. Toilet paper, diapers, detergents, chow. That is man's sacred circle, and our mission is not only to discover it, seize it, and map it but to make it beautiful, to transform it into song. Thanks to our influence, toilet paper is almost exclusively pink, and that is a highly edifying fact, which, my dear and anxious lady, I would recommend that you contemplate seriously."

"But that's desolation, desolation!" said the lady, her voice wavering like the lament of a woman raped. "It's just desolation with makeup on! We put makeup on desolation!"

"Yes, precisely," said Leroy, and in that "precisely" Chantal heard the pleasure he got from the refined lady's lament.

"But then where is the grandeur of life? If we're condemned to chow and coitus and toilet paper, who are we? And if that's all we're capable of, what pride can we take in the fact that we are, as they tell us, free beings?"

Chantal looked at the lady and thought that this was the ideal victim of an orgy. She imagined a scene where people undressed her, chained up her old, refined body, and forced her to recite her naïve verities in a loud lament, while in front of her they would all be copulating and exposing themselves. . . .

Leroy interrupted Chantal's fantasies: "Freedom? As you live out your desolation, you can be either unhappy or happy. Having that choice is what constitutes your freedom. You're free to melt your own individuality into the cauldron of the multitude either with a feeling of defeat or with euphoria. Our choice, my dear lady, is euphoria."

Chantal felt a smile take shape on her face. She paid serious mind to what Leroy had just said: our only freedom is choosing between bitterness and pleasure. Since the insignificance of all things is our lot, we should not bear it as an affliction but learn to enjoy it. She watched Leroy's impassive face, the perverse and charming intelligence that radiated from it. She watched him with affection but without desire, and she told herself (as if she were sweeping aside her reverie of a moment past) that he had long ago transsubstantiated all his male energy into the force of his trenchant logic and into the authority he wielded over his work group. She imagined their exit from the train: while Leroy continued to scare the adoring lady with his talk, Chantal would vanish discreetly into a phone booth and thence give them all the slip.

44

The Japanese, the Americans, the Spanish, the Russians, all of them with cameras around their necks, leave the train, and Jean-Marc tries not to lose sight of Chantal. The broad human flood suddenly shrinks and disappears below the platform down an escalator. At the bottom of the escalator, in the main waiting room, a film crew rushes forward, followed by a mob of gawkers, and blocks his way. The passengers from the train are forced to stop. There is applause and shouting as some children come down a side staircase. They are all wearing helmets, helmets in various colors, as if they are a sports team, little motorcycle or ski racers. It's they who are being

147

filmed. Jean-Marc stands on tiptoe hoping to spot Chantal over the crowd's heads. At last, he sees her. She is on the far side of the column of children, in a telephone booth. Receiver to her ear, she is talking. Jean-Marc struggles to cut himself a path. He jostles a cameraman who, in a fury, gives him a kick. Jean-Marc jabs the man with an elbow, and he just misses dropping his camera. A policeman approaches and orders Jean-Marc to wait till the shooting is done. Just then, for a second or two, his eyes meet Chantal's as she leaves the phone booth. Again he pushes forward to get through the crowd. The policeman twists his arm in a grip so painful that Jean-Marc doubles over and loses sight of Chantal.

The last helmeted child has gone by and only then does the cop loosen his grip and let him go. He looks toward the phone booth but it is empty. Near him a group of French people has stopped; he recognizes Chantal's colleagues.

"Where is Chantal?" he asks a girl.

She answers in a reproachful tone: "You're the one who should know! She was in such great spirits! But when we got off the train she disappeared!"

Another woman, fatter, is upset: "I saw you on

the train. You were signaling her. I saw it all. You ruined everything."

Leroy's voice breaks in: "Let's go!"

The girl asks: "What about Chantal?"

"She knows the address."

"This gentleman," says the refined lady with ring-covered fingers, "is looking for her too."

Jean-Marc is sure that Leroy knows him by sight as he does Leroy. "Hello."

"Hello," Leroy answers, and he smiles. "I saw you tussling. One against the horde."

Jean-Marc thinks he hears some sympathy in the man's voice. In his distress it's like a hand offered and he wants to take it; it's like a spark that, in a moment, promises him friendship; friendship between two men who, without knowing each other, simply out of the pleasure of a sudden mutual sympathy, are prepared to help each other. It's as if a beautiful dream were descending on him.

Confident, he says: "Can you tell me the name of your hotel? I'd like to phone and see if Chantal's there."

Leroy is silent, then he asks: "She didn't give it to you?"

"No."

"In that case, excuse me," he says kindly, almost with regret. "I can't give it to you."

Snuffed out, the spark fell back down, and Jean-Marc suddenly felt a pain in the shoulder bruised by the cop's grip. Bereft, he left the station. Not knowing where to go, he set off, walking wherever the streets led.

As he walks, he pulls the banknotes from his pocket and counts them again. He has enough for the return trip but nothing more. If he decides to, he can leave right away. He'll be in Paris tonight. Obviously, that would be the most sensible solution. What is he going to do here? He has nothing to do. And yet he cannot leave. He'll never decide to leave. He cannot leave London if Chantal is here.

But since he must save his money for the return trip, he cannot take a hotel room, he cannot eat, not even a sandwich. Where is he going to sleep? All at once he knows that the assertion he often made to Chantal is finally about to be confirmed: that his deepest vocation is to be a marginal person, a marginal person who has lived comfortably, true, but only under completely uncertain and temporary circumstances. Now suddenly here is his true self, thrown back among those he belongs with: among the poor who have no roof to shelter their destitution.

He recalls his arguments with Chantal and feels the childish need to have her here before him just to tell her: See, I was right, it wasn't a fake claim, I really am who I am, a marginal person, homeless, a bum.

45

Evening had fallen, and the air had chilled. He took a street lined on one side by a row of houses, on the other by a square enclosed in a black grillwork fence. There, on the sidewalk that ran along the square, stood a wooden bench; he sat down. He was exhausted and wanted to put his legs up on the bench and stretch out. He thought: that's certainly how it starts. One day a person puts his legs up on a bench, then night comes and he falls asleep. That's how it happens that one fine day a person joins the tramps and turns into one of them.

Therefore, calling on all his energies, he mastered his fatigue and remained sitting up very straight, like a good pupil in a classroom. Behind him were trees and in front of him, across the road, were houses; they were all alike, white, three-story, with two columns at the door and four windows on each floor. He looked carefully at each passerby on that little-traveled street. He was determined to stay right there until he should see Chantal. Waiting was the only thing he could do for her, for them both.

Abruptly, some thirty meters off to the right, all the windows light up in one of the houses, and inside it someone pulls red curtains closed. He reckons that some fashionable folk have come for a party. But he is astonished not to have seen anyone go in; have they been there all along and are they just turning on the lights now? Or had he perhaps dozed off unawares and not seen them arrive? Good God, what if he'd missed Chantal while he slept? Instantly, he is thunderstruck by the suspicion of an orgy; he hears the words "You know very well why London"; and that "you know very well" suddenly appears in a wholly other light: London, the city of the Englishman, the British fellow, Britannicus; it was him she was phoning from the railroad station, and it was for him she had escaped Leroy, her colleagues, all of them.

Jealousy grips him, huge and harrowing—not the abstract, mental jealousy he had experienced standing at the open wardrobe and asking himself the theoretical question about Chantal's capacity to betray him, but jealousy as he had known it in his youth, jealousy that pierces the body, that wounds it, that is unbearable. He imagines Chantal giving herself to other men, submissive and devoted, and he can no longer contain himself. He rises and runs toward the house. The door, bright white, is lighted by a lantern. He turns the handle, the door opens, he enters, sees a staircase with a red carpet, hears the sound of voices above, goes up, reaches the big second-floor landing whose whole width is taken up by a long rack holding not only coats but also (and this is a fresh blow to the heart) some women's dresses and a few men's shirts. In a rage, he plunges through all these clothes and is just reaching a big double door, also white, when a heavy hand lands on his sore shoulder. He turns and feels on his cheek the hot breath of a brawny man, in a T-shirt, with tattooed arms, who speaks to him in English.

He struggles to shake off that hand, which hurts him more and more and is pushing him toward the staircase. There, still trying to resist, he loses his balance and only at the last moment manages to clutch at the banister. Vanquished, he walks slowly down the staircase. The tattooed man follows him and when Jean-Marc stops, hesitating, at the front door, he shouts something in English and, with a raised arm, orders him to leave.

46

The image of an orgy had stayed with Chantal for a long time, in her turbulent dreams, in her imagery, even in her conversations with Jean-Marc, who had told her one day (one day so distant): I'd really like to be there with you, but on one condition: that at the moment of climax each of the participants would turn into an animal—a sheep, a cow, a goat—and the Dionysian orgy would become a pastoral where we'd be the only ones left among the beasts, like a shepherd and shepherdess. (That idyllic fantasy amused her: the poor orgiasts hurrying to the mansion of debauchery unaware that they'll be leaving there as cows.)

She is surrounded by naked people, and right now she would prefer sheep to humans. Not wanting to see anyone anymore, she closes her eyes; but behind her lids she sees them still, their organs rising up, shrinking down, thick, thin. It makes her think of a field with earthworms rearing upright, bending, twisting, falling back. Then she sees not earthworms but snakes; she is repelled and nonetheless still aroused. Except that this arousal does not stir the desire to make love again, on the contrary, the more aroused she is the more she is repelled by her own arousal for making her aware that her body belongs not to her own self but to this boggy field, this field of worms and snakes.

She opens her eyes: from the adjoining room comes a woman, in her direction; she halts in the wide-open doorway, and as if she proposed to tear Chantal away from this male inanity, this kingdom of earthworms, she surveys Chantal with a seductive gaze. She is tall, gorgeously built, with blonde hair around a beautiful face. Just as Chantal is about to respond to her mute invitation, the blonde rounds her lips and extrudes some saliva. Chantal sees that mouth as if magnified by a powerful glass: the saliva is white and full of tiny bubbles; the woman moves the saliva foam in and out as if to entice Chantal, as if to promise her tender, wet kisses in which one of the women would dissolve into the other.

Chantal watches the saliva bead and tremble and ooze on those lips, and her disgust becomes nausea. She turns away to hide it. But from behind her, the blonde snatches her hand. Chantal breaks free and takes a few steps to get away. Feeling the blonde's hand again on her body, she starts to run. She hears the breathing of her tormentor, who probably sees her flight as an erotic game. She is trapped: the more she tries to escape, the more she stimulates the blonde, who attracts more tormentors to chase after her like quarry.

She turns down a corridor and hears steps behind her. The bodies pursuing her repel her so much that her disgust swiftly turns to terror: she runs as if she had to save her life. The corridor is long and it ends at a door that opens onto a small tiled room with another door in one corner; she opens it, and shuts it behind her.

In the darkness, she leans against a wall to catch her breath; then she feels around the door and turns on the light. It is a broom closet: vacuum cleaner, mops, aprons. And on the floor, upon a pile of rags, a dog lies rolled up in a ball. No longer hearing voices from outside, she thinks: the animals' time has come, and I'm saved. Aloud, she asks the dog: "Which one of those men are you?"

Suddenly she is unsettled by what she's said. My God, she wonders, where did I get the idea that at the end of the orgy people would turn into animals?

It is strange: she has no idea at all where she got that notion. She searches her memory and finds nothing. She just feels a sweet sensation that calls to mind no specific memory, an enigmatic sensation, inexplicably cheering, like a greeting from afar.

Abruptly, roughly, the door opens. A black woman has come in, small, in a green smock. She throws Chantal a glance, unsurprised, curt, contemptuous. Chantal steps aside to allow the woman to take the big vacuum cleaner and leave with it. She has thereby stepped closer to the dog, who shows his fangs and growls. Terror grips her again; she goes out.

47

She was in the corridor and had only one thought: to find the landing where her clothes were hanging on a rack. But the doors whose handles she tried were all locked. At last, by the open double door, she entered the salon; it seemed strangely large and empty: the black woman in the green smock was already at work with the big vacuum cleaner. Of the whole crowd from the evening, there remained only a few gentlemen, who stood talking, their voices low; they were dressed and paid no attention to Chantal who, noticing her suddenly inappropriate nakedness, watched them timidly. Another gentleman, around seventy years old, in a white robe and slippers, went over and spoke to them.

She racked her brains to think how she could get out, but in that very different atmosphere, with that unexpected depopulation, the layout of the rooms seemed almost transfigured, and she was unable to get her bearings. She saw the wide-open door to the adjoining room where the blonde with spit on her mouth had made the approach to her; she went through it; the room was empty; she stopped and looked around for a door out; there was none.

She returned to the salon and saw that meanwhile the gentlemen had left. Why had she not paid more attention? She could have followed them! Only the septuagenarian in the robe was there. Their gazes met and she recognized him; with a sudden rush of confidence, she went over to him: "I phoned you, remember? You told me to come, but when I got here I didn't see you!"

"I know, I know, excuse me, I don't join in these children's games anymore," he said, genially but without paying her much attention. He went to the windows and opened them one after the other. A strong breeze blew through the room.

"I'm so happy to find someone I know," said Chantal, agitated.

"I've got to get rid of all this stench."

"Tell me how to get to the landing. All my things are there."

"Be patient," he said, and he went into a corner of the salon where a leftover chair stood; he brought it to her: "Sit here. I'll take care of you as soon as I'm free."

The chair is set down in the center of the salon. Docilely, she sits. The septuagenarian goes over

159

to the black woman and disappears with her into the next room. Now the vacuum cleaner is roaring in there; through the noise, Chantal hears the voice of the septuagenarian giving orders and then a few hammer blows. A hammer? she wonders. Who's working with a hammer here? She hasn't seen anyone! Someone must have come! But what door did he get in by?

The breeze lifts the red curtains beside the windows. Naked on her chair, Chantal is cold. Again she hears the hammer blows, and, frightened, she understands: they are nailing shut the doors! She will never get out of here! A feeling of enormous danger sweeps through her. She rises from her chair and takes three or four steps, but not knowing where to go, she stops. She wants to shout for help. But who can help her? In that moment of extreme anxiety, she glimpses again the image of a man struggling against the crowd to get to her. Someone is twisting his arm behind his back. She cannot see his face, sees only his contorted figure. Good Lord, she wishes she could remember him a little more clearly, call up his features, but she can't manage it, she knows only that it is the man who loves her and that's all that matters to her now. She has seen him here in this city, he can't be far. She wants to find him as soon as possible. But how? The doors are nailed shut! Then she sees the red curtain fluttering at a window. The windows! They're open! She has to go to the window! Shout into the street! She can even jump out, if the window isn't too high! Another hammer blow. And another. It's now or never. Time is working against her. This is her last chance to act.

48

He came back to the bench, barely visible in the darkness between the only two streetlamps, very far apart from each other.

He made to sit down and heard a howl. He jumped; a man who meantime had taken over the bench swore at him. He went off without protesting. That's it, he said to himself, that's my new status; I'm even going to have to fight for a little spot to sleep in.

He stopped across the street from where the lantern hanging between the two columns lit the white door of the house he had been thrown out of two minutes earlier. He sat on the sidewalk and leaned back against the grillwork fence that surrounded the park.

Then rain, a fine rain, began to fall. He pulled up the collar of his jacket and watched the house.

Abruptly, one by one, the windows open. The red curtains, pulled back to the sides, float in the breeze and let him see through to the illuminated white ceiling. What does that mean? The party is over? But no one's come out! A few minutes ago he was searing on the fire of jealousy and now it is only fear he feels, only fear for Chantal. He wants to do everything for her but he does not know what should be done and that's what is intolerable: he does not know how to help her and yet he is the only one who can help her, he, he alone, because she has nobody else in the world, nobody anywhere in the world.

His face wet with tears, he stands up, takes a few steps toward the house, and calls out her name.

49

With another chair in hand, the septuagenarian stops in front of Chantal: "Where do you want to go?"

Startled, she sees him before her, and in this moment of great consternation a strong wave of heat rises from the depths of her body, fills her belly, her chest, covers her face. She is in flames. She is utterly naked, she is utterly red, and the man's gaze resting on her body is making her feel every iota of her burning nakedness. Automatically, she puts her hand over her breast as if to hide it. Inside her body, the flames quickly consume her courage and her rebellion. Suddenly she feels tired. Suddenly she feels weak.

He takes her by the arm, leads her to her chair, and sets his own chair right in front of her. They are sitting alone, face-to-face, close together, in the middle of the empty salon.

The cold breeze embraces Chantal's sweating body. She shivers, and in a thin, supplicating voice, she asks: "Can't I get out of here?"

"And why don't you want to stay here with me, Anne?" he asks her reproachfully.

"Anne?" She is icy with horror: "Why do you call me Anne?"

"Isn't that your name?"

"I'm not Anne!"

"But I've always known you by the name Anne!"

From the next room a few hammer blows were again heard; he turned his head in that direction as if he hesitated to interfere. She took advantage of that moment of isolation to try to understand: she is naked, but they keep on stripping her! Stripping her of her self! Stripping her of her destiny! They'll give her a different name and then abandon her among strangers to whom she can never explain who she is.

She no longer has any hope of getting out of this place. The doors are nailed shut. She must, modestly, begin at the beginning. The beginning is her name. What she wants to achieve first, as an indispensable minimum, is to have this man call her by her name, her real name. That's the first thing she'll ask of him. Demand of him. But no sooner does she set herself this goal than she realizes that her name is somehow blocked in her mind; she does not remember it.

That fills her with panic, but she knows that

her life is at stake and that to defend herself, to fight, she must at all costs keep her head; with furious concentration, she strains to remember: she was given three baptismal names, yes, three, she has been using only one of them, that she knows, but what were those three names, and which one did she retain? Good Lord, she must have heard that name thousands of times!

The thought of the man who loved her returns to mind. If he were here, he would call her by her name. Maybe, if she managed to remember his face, she could imagine the mouth pronouncing her name. That seems a good trail to follow: getting to her name by way of that man. She tries to imagine him, and, once again, she sees a figure struggling in a crowd. The image is pale, fleeting, she strains to hold on to it, hold it and deepen it, stretch it back toward the past: where did he come from, that man? how did he come to be in that crowd? why was he fighting?

She strains to stretch that memory, and a garden appears, large, and a country house, where among many people she makes out a small man, puny, and she remembers having had a child with him, a child she knows nothing about except that he is dead. . . .

"Where have you wandered off to, Anne?"

She raises her head and sees someone old sitting on a chair facing her and looking at her.

"My child is dead," she says. The memory is too weak; for that very reason she says it loud; she thinks to make it more real that way; she thinks to hold on to it that way, as a bit of her life slipping away from her.

He leans toward her, takes her hands, and says calmly in a voice full of encouragement: "Anne, forget your child, forget your dead, think about life!"

He smiles at her. Then he waves broadly, as if to indicate something immense and sublime: "Life! Life, Anne, life!"

The smile and the gesture fill her with dread. She stands. She trembles. Her voice trembles: "What life? What do you call life?"

The question she has unthinkingly asked calls up another one: what if this was already death? what if this is what death is?

She shoves away the chair, which rolls across the salon and hits the wall. She wants to shout but cannot find a word. A long, inarticulate "ahhhh" bursts from her mouth.

50

"Chantal! Chantal! Chantal!"

He was clasping her body as it shuddered with the cry.

"Wake up! It's not real!"

She trembled in his arms, and he told her many times more that it was not real.

She repeated after him: "No, it isn't real, it isn't real," and slowly, very slowly, she grew quiet.

And I ask myself: who was dreaming? Who dreamed this story? Who imagined it? She? He? Both of them? Each one for the other? And starting when did their real life change into this treacherous fantasy? When the train drove down under the Channel? Earlier? The morning she announced her departure for London? Even earlier than that? The day in the graphologist's office, when she met the waiter from the café in the Normandy town? Or earlier still? When Jean-Marc sent her the first letter? But did he really send those letters? Or did he only imagine writing them? At what exact moment did the real turn into the unreal, reality into reverie? Where was the border? Where is the border?

51

I see their two heads, in profile, lit by the light of a little bedside lamp: Jean-Marc's head, its nape on a pillow; Chantal's head leaning close above him.

She said: "I'll never let you out of my sight again. I'm going to keep on watching you and never stop."

And after a pause: "I get scared when my eye blinks. Scared that during that second when my gaze goes out, a snake or a rat or another man could slip into your place."

He tried to raise himself a little to touch her with his lips.

She shook her head: "No, I just want to watch you."

And then: "I'm going to leave the lamp on all night. Every night."

COMPLETED IN FRANCE, IN AUTUMN 1996